Rave Reviews for
Erle Stanley GARDNER!

I went to the door, opened it wide and was about to enter the room when I heard steps in the outer office.

I ran to the window and looked out. There was a car parked just behind mine. I couldn't see it too clearly but it was a big shiny car.

I pushed aside the curtains on the open window, eased myself over the sill and dropped to the ground. I started walking toward my car, then thought better of it and sprinted.

I jumped in the car, started the motor and eased into motion as noiselessly as possible.

Someone yelled.

I could see a man's frame silhouetted against the light in the room, standing in the open window from which I had made my departure.

"Hey, you!" he yelled. "Come back here! Stop where you are!"

I stepped on the throttle.

I had a blurred glimpse of the man climbing through the window and running across the lawn toward his car. Then I skidded into a turn at the end of the driveway, hit the paved road and pushed down the foot throttle.

I had gone about half a mile before I picked up the head-lights in my rearview mirror.

I gave the car everything it had...

Shills Can't
CASH CHIPS

by Erle Stanley Gardner

WRITING UNDER THE NAME 'A. A. FAIR'

A HARD CASE CRIME NOVEL

A HARD CASE CRIME BOOK
(HCC-145)
First Hard Case Crime edition: October 2020

Published by

Titan Books
A division of Titan Publishing Group Ltd
144 Southwark Street
London SE1 0UP

in collaboration with Winterfall LLC

This book is a work of fiction. Names, characters, places, and incidents either are the products of the author's imagination or are used fictitiously, and any resemblance to actual events or persons, living or dead, is entirely coincidental.

Print edition ISBN 978-1-78565-6361
E-book ISBN 978-1-78565-6378

Design direction by Max Phillips
www.maxphillips.net

Typeset by Swordsmith Productions

The name "Hard Case Crime" and the Hard Case Crime logo are trademarks of Winterfall LLC. Hard Case Crime books are selected and edited by Charles Ardai.

Printed and bound by CPI Group (UK) Ltd, Croydon, CR0 4YY

Visit us on the web at www.HardCaseCrime.com

SHILLS CAN'T CASH CHIPS

1

I walked across the reception room of COOL & LAM, INVESTI-
GATORS, opened the door of my private office. Elsie Brand, my
secretary, looked up with an expression I had come to know.

"What is it, Elsie?" I asked. "Good or bad?"

"What?"

"What you wanted to tell me."

"How did you know I had something to tell you?"

"The expression on your face."

"Don't I have *any* secrets from you?" she asked.

I smiled at her. She became flustered and said, "If you had
time, Donald, to step down the hall with me, I...I wanted to
show you something."

"I have the time," I said. "Let's go."

We left my office, walked across the reception room, down
the hall, and Elsie led the way to the storage closets, took a key,
unlocked the door of closet number eight and switched on the
light.

These storage closets were in a dead windowless space in the
building, and our closet had been used as a catchall for old junk
that should have been thrown away. Now it had been neatly
segregated into shelves, and the shelves were lined with scrapbooks.

"What the heck!" I said.

Elsie was looking at me, her eyes filled with pride. "I've been
wanting to surprise you," she said.

"You've surprised me. Now tell me about it."

"Well," she said, "you've been having me cut out all of those crime clippings and it's been a job trying to find some way of filing them."

"I didn't want you to file them," I said, "just to keep them handy so I could put my hand on the more recent ones."

"Well," she said, "you can always find anything you want now. For instance, here's Volume A. That is crimes of violence. Numbers one to one hundred are murders for motives of jealousy. Numbers one hundred to two hundred are murders committed in connection with armed robberies. There are ten divisions in all.

"Now I've got a cross-index system over here of weapons. Murders with guns, murders with knives, murders with poison.

"Then this next volume, Volume B, is the robbery book. Volume C is larceny. D is—"

Bertha Cool's harsh, rasping voice behind us said, "What in hell goes on here?"

Elsie Brand gave a little gasp.

I turned to face my indignant partner, her eyes diamond-hard, glittering, her face dark with anger.

"My reference library," I said.

"What in hell do you want with a reference library?"

"I want to refer to it."

Bertha snorted. "They told me you and Elsie were lolligagging down the hall. I wondered what you two were up to...."

Bertha grabbed one of the volumes, looked through it and said to Elsie, "So *that's* what you've been doing with all of your time!"

Elsie started to say something but I moved in between her and Bertha Cool. "That's what she's been doing with her *spare* time," I said. "And in case you've forgotten it, having the information available on outstanding, unsolved crimes has enabled us to cooperate with the police and get us out of a couple of rather tight spots."

"You're always getting in tight spots," Bertha flared. "Then you squeak out by the skin of your eyeteeth and—"

"And leave our bank account in better shape than it was when we started," I told her, getting mad. "Now if you have any complaints, go back to your office, make them in the form of a written memo and hand them to Elsie. We'll file them in our complaint department, which, in case you are interested, is the wastebasket."

"Now Donald," Bertha said, "don't be like that."

"Like what?"

"You're getting mad."

"Getting mad!" I said. "I *am* mad."

"Now Donald, don't be difficult. I was looking for you for a particular reason and I was impatient when no one answered the phone in your office."

"Well, Elsie was showing me the new filing system."

Bertha said, "It looks like hell when I have a client in my office and want to bring in my partner to introduce him and can't get an answer on the telephone. No secretary, no partner, no nothing—so I come to hunt you up. Here's a client sitting in the office, impatient as hell, and you folks smooching down here in the storage closet."

"We weren't smooching," I said.

"You could have been," Bertha said, "for all I knew. The way you two look at each other—"

"Now look," I told Bertha, "if you have a client who's impatiently waiting in your office, we'd better go take care of him. If you want to comment about our personal relations, you can put that in the form of a memo which—"

"All right, all right," Bertha said irritably. "Come on....Elsie, you close up this damned closet. Donald, let's go talk with our client. This is the kind of work we want. This is respectable work."

Bertha turned and started waddling down the corridor, a hundred and sixty-five pounds of bulldog tenacity, hair-trigger temper, greediness and shrewd observation; an explosive combination of characteristics that were rendered somewhat less obnoxious by an underlying loyalty when the chips were down.

At that, our partnership would probably have split up long ago if it hadn't been so profitable. Money in the bank represented the most persuasive argument in Bertha's life, and when it came to a showdown where the dissolution of the partnership was threatened, Bertha could always manage to control her irascible temper.

As I caught up with Bertha she said, "This is an insurance company. They've had their eye on us for a while. It's the kind of business that there's money in, Donald, not this wild-eyed sharpshooting you've been doing."

"We've made money out of sharpshooting," I reminded her. "Lots of it."

"Too damned much," Bertha said. "It scares me. We take too many risks. This job Hawley has for us is just the first of many."

"All right," I said. "Who's Hawley?"

Bertha paused in front of the door to the outer office, briefing me momentarily before she turned the knob.

"Lamont Hawley," she said, "is head of the Claims Department of Consolidated Interinsurance. He'll tell you all about it. Now Donald, be nice to him. This is the sort of stuff we need."

"What's in it for us?" I asked.

"A hundred a day and expenses, with a guarantee of ten days as a minimum, and we furnish whatever operatives are required to cover the job."

"How many operatives can we furnish at that price?"

"One," she said, her eyes boring into mine. "You. And be damned certain that that's *all* we need!"

Bertha jerked the door open and barged across the reception room and opened the door of her private office.

The man who got up as we entered was tall, sparebuilt, shrewd-eyed and long-featured. He was a typical detail man in the higher brackets. He could coordinate facts, figures and people and come up with the answers.

"My partner, Donald Lam," Bertha Cool said. "Donald, this is Lamont Hawley, Consolidated Interinsurance."

Hawley shook hands. His long fingers wrapped around my hand. His lip smile was a meaningless concession to the conventions. His eyes didn't smile.

"I've heard a lot about you, Mr. Lam," he said.

"Good, bad or indifferent?"

"Good. Very good, indeed. You have created quite an impression. I had expected a…a larger man."

"Don't bother to beat around the bush," Bertha Cool said, heaving her bulk into the squeaky swivel chair behind her desk. "Everybody gets fooled by Donald. He's young and little but the bastard has brains.

"Now, I've told Donald what the deal is and it's okay. I handle the financial end of the business. He supervises the outdoor work. You go ahead and tell Donald about the case."

Hawley kept looking me over as though a little reluctant to accept me at face value, but at length seated himself, took a filing jacket from his briefcase, put the filing jacket on his knee and then didn't refer to it but rattled off the facts and figures from memory.

"Carter J. Holgate, a real estate sharpshooter," he said. "A money-maker with a horror of being stuck for damages in an accident, carries unlimited public liability insurance with us.

On August thirteenth, was driving north in the city of Colinda, when he came to a traffic signal.

"He has admitted to us that he was tired and that he may have been inattentive. He had been following a light car through the city. They approached a traffic intersection at Seventh and Main Streets. The signal light changed to red, the car ahead of Holgate stopped, Holgate says very abruptly, but we can't establish this by any other evidence.

"Holgate smashed into the rear of the car ahead. That car was driven by Vivian Deshler, Apartment six-nineteen Miramar Apartments, Colinda, California; age, twenty-six, blond, five feet four; weight, a hundred and twelve; apparently a divorcee living on a lump-sum property alimony settlement that is about used up. Her car was a fast sports job, but low and light.

"She claims a whiplash injury to the neck.

"Of course you know a whiplash injury is an insurance company's nightmare. There's no question on earth but what they can be exceedingly serious and that the symptoms can be delayed for some time. On the other hand, there's virtually no way of checking. A person says, I've got a headache, how are you going to prove she doesn't have a headache? You can't do it.

"There's no question at all about the liability of our insured. He was road-weary and tells us confidentially he'd hoped he could get around the string of traffic ahead. He'd speeded up to make it around, found out he couldn't, had swung back into line going much faster than the traffic and just failed to see the red light at the intersection ahead. His reaction time was slowed down so that he crashed into the rear end of the car in front of him, and of course it would have to be a light car."

"All right," I said, "where do we come in on this?"

"In injuries of this sort," Hawley said, "we try to find out something about the background of the injured person. We like to find out who they are, where they came from, what they're doing, and we are particularly concerned with trying to find out how their day-to-day activities fit into the picture of serious injuries.

"In other words, a young, attractive woman gets on the stand and shows lots of nylon to the jury. She smiles at them and then begins to describe her symptoms. Her voice shows that she's suffering, her smile indicates she's bravely bearing up as she faces the prospects of ruined life. She tells about the headaches, about the periods of sleeplessness, about her increasing nervousness, and all the rest of it.

"Now, quite obviously, if we can take her on cross-examination and say, 'Well now, let's take a typical day in your life, Miss Deshler. Let's take September nineteenth of the present year, for instance. You complain of sleeplessness, yet you didn't bring in the newspaper and milk on your doorstep until ten-fifteen. Then at eleven-ten you left your apartment and went to the beach. You were surf swimming during the afternoon. In the evening you and your escort went to a dance. You drove from the dance up on the ocean highway, parked where you could look out over the ocean and were there for two hours and a half. Then your escort drove you home, went into your apartment and was there for an hour and forty minutes.'

"Then we show motion pictures of her in a tight-fitting bathing suit running along the beach, turning her head and laughing invitingly at her escort. We show her in the surf. We show her on the beach displaying her figure to advantage.

"By the time we get done showing the motion pictures and cross-examining the young woman, the jurors feel her life hasn't been unduly circumscribed. Her activities haven't been interfered with *too* greatly."

"Now, wait a minute," I said, "do you want me to start dogging this girl around, getting motion pictures of her when she goes to the beach, finding out what time she opens the apartment door to get the newspaper, watching her boyfriend—"

"No, no," Hawley interrupted. "That's highly specialized work. We have our own methods of getting that information and we have our own trick cameras with telephoto lenses. Also, Mr. Lam, you want to remember the way I approached the subject.

"Notice that I say that on cross-examination we say, 'Now, Miss Deshler, let's take a typical day of your life,' and then we pull out the list of things that happened on that particular day.

"Now, note that we don't ask her if that *was* a typical day in her life. Instead, our attorney says, 'Let's take a typical day in your life,' and then he starts listing all of the things that happened on this particular day. He gives the impression that we've been covering her activities in minute detail from the time the suit was filed until the case came to trial. Actually we may only have a couple of days of coverage and those days may have been days of unusual activity, but we lead up to it by saying, 'Let's take a typical day in your life,' and then start bringing out motion picture films and voluminous records. We convey the impression we want and at the same time frighten the witness, because she doesn't know just how much we know. In other words, she probably feels that we *have* been covering her activities day by day, minute by minute, and night by night."

"I see," I said.

"Now, don't act as though we were stealing candy from babies, Lam," Hawley said with a magnetic, keen-eyed smile. "We're dealing with a racket. This whole thing has become highly specialized.

"Take, for instance, this Vivian Deshler. She may be the isolated individual we're working on at the moment but remember that she isn't really isolated. She has a whole organization behind her. She has an attorney at law who—"

"Who *is* her attorney?" I interrupted.

"We don't know," Hawley said. "She hasn't filed suit as yet. She's made a claim, and of course we'd like to settle the claim without having suit filed. The point I'm trying to make is that she has an attorney, even if we don't know who he is as yet. The attorney is one who has specialized in representing plaintiffs in automobile accident cases. He's a member of an organization that gives mutual aid.

"In other words, any time one attorney finds out some little trick that gets a bigger verdict out of a jury, he passes that on to all the members in the association. Any time someone gets a whopping big verdict for a broken leg, that information is flashed around to all the members of the organization and right away that establishes a new standard for a broken leg. And so it goes."

"So you're fighting the devil with fire?" I asked.

"Well, we don't look at it in exactly that way," Hawley said. "We simply have to protect ourselves. Otherwise there wouldn't be any automobile driving or any automobile insurance. Premiums would go up to such a point that people simply couldn't afford to carry insurance."

"Let's get back to what you want me to do," I said.

"We want you to locate Vivian Deshler."

"But I thought you said she lived—"

"We know where she *did* live, but we don't know where she is now. She made a claim. She was very helpful. She agreed to let our doctor examine her. She permitted us to take X rays. She was most cooperative and friendly and she said she didn't want to fix the amount of her claim just at present, that she had plenty of time before the statute of limitations would cause the suit to outlaw, and that she wanted to see how her injuries responded to treatment and all that."

"She sounds very levelheaded," I said.

"Very levelheaded indeed. In fact she has a smooth touch—almost a professional touch. She did state that she would be willing to accept a thirty-thousand-dollar settlement and let it go at that—and then she simply moved out of the picture. We don't know where she went.

"Now, we'd like very much to find her. It bothers us when something of this sort happens. This claim, you understand, Mr. Lam, is one where we're going to have to admit liability. It's simply a question of how much we're going to have to pay in order to get a settlement.

"Now then, we want your agency to find Vivian Deshler."

"You have a pretty good investigative department," I said. "Why don't you use it?"

"We're busy with other things and…well, frankly, Lam, we tried all the usual procedures and they didn't work. We don't know where she is. We can't find her. We want her."

I said, "Look, this is your business. You're specialists. How do you expect us to find this girl if your organization is unable to get a clue?"

Hawley said, "We think that you're just that much better than we are."

Bertha beamed.

I said, "Come again."

"I beg your pardon?" Hawley said.

I said, "Express that in terms that I can understand."

Hawley said, "Well, I'll put it *this* way. We have one clue to Vivian Deshler. She has one friend in Colinda and that friend, as it happens, lives in the same apartment house, the Miramar

Apartments. Her name is Doris Ashley. She is twenty-eight, a brunette, with a very good figure, and no apparent source of income that we have been able to ascertain.

"Doris Ashley is very friendly with Dudley H. Bedford, a man of about thirty-five, who is reputed to have made money buying and selling real estate and apparently has been rather good at it.

"Now, our organization is one where the personnel is advanced upon merit in terms of seniority, and since the position of an investigator requires a great deal of experience and tact, the positions are not filled by the younger men.

"All routine contacts with Doris Ashley have failed and…well, we had a staff meeting, and decided that a younger, more personable operative who had no known connection with our company might get the desired information."

Hawley beamed at me.

Bertha Cool said, "My God, what Donald does to women! They cry on his shoulder; they unburden themselves completely. If you want a girl turned inside out, that's the brainy little bastard that can do it."

"I'm satisfied he can," Hawley said.

"I don't think I'm going to like this," I said.

"Oh, you'll love it!" Bertha exclaimed. "It's a challenge, Donald."

I kept my eyes on Hawley. "Look," I said, "if I go at this, I'm going at it in my own way. You want to locate Vivian Deshler, is that right?"

"That's right."

"You don't care how it's done, just so it's done."

"We have exhausted the obvious ways," he reminded me.

"I understand all that, but the object of our employment is to locate Vivian Deshler, right?"

"Right."

"All right, here's the only way I'll work on it. I'll give it a once-over at a hundred a day and expenses. At any time I don't want to go ahead we're free to quit."

"We wouldn't like it that way, Lam."

"We wouldn't like it any other way," I told him.

Bertha started to say something. My glance warned her to a reluctant silence.

Hawley sighed. "Okay, it's a deal."

"Okay, now tell me about Doris Ashley," I said.

For the first time, Hawley looked at his notes. "She drives an Oldsmobile, last year's model, license number RTD nine-thirteen. It's a wide-door club coupe. She shops at the Colinda Supermarket, does her own cooking in the apartment except when she's invited out at night and that's mostly every night."

"Dudley Bedford?" I asked.

Hawley nodded.

"What about the Miramar Apartments?" I asked. "Does it have a garage?"

"No, there's a vacant lot to the north of the apartment house and they use that as a parking lot on a catch-as-catch-can basis. There are usually parking facilities available on the street in front of the apartment house."

"Doris Ashley a late sleeper?" I asked.

"Very late," he said. "She gets up a little before noon each day, goes shopping about two-thirty in the afternoon, apparently right after breakfast. We haven't been able to find out too much about her. There's an atmosphere of secretiveness, of mystery, about the whole setup that bothers us. Frankly, Mr. Lam, we're willing to spend a little more than we expect to save on the settlement because we don't like these things. We don't like cases that don't follow a pattern. We have to run our business on a basis of averages. That's the way we figure our premiums. That's the way we like to pay off our losses."

"I see," I said.

Hawley got up and shook hands. "I've left my private unlisted telephone number with Mrs. Cool," he said. "You can count on cooperation from our organization on anything you want, but of course I must warn you against having any visible contact with us. As the insurance carrier, we assume we have been spotted and anything we might try to do would be anticipated."

"I see," I told him. "Well, thanks a lot. We'll get busy."

He bowed to Bertha, started out, paused in the doorway. "I may as well tell you, Lam, we think there's an element of danger involved."

"Personal?"

"Yes."

"How do you figure that?"

He smiled. "We have had an interesting and anonymous tip-off on the telephone," he said. "You'd better be careful."

He stepped out and closed the door behind him.

Bertha Cool's face was wreathed in smiles.

"Isn't it wonderful, Donald?" she said. "Here's a big insurance organization with its own investigative staff and when it gets to a really difficult case they turn to us."

I said nothing.

"And of course," Bertha said, "we're not dumb enough to fall for all this line of chatter about *why* they're willing to spend money to get the information they want. Something in the case is worrying them. They've made a pass at this jane, got a jolt, and they're scared."

"That's for certain," I told her. "Well, I'll get going and look the ground over."

"Keep me posted," Bertha said. "This is an important case. And don't frighten the client with those whopping big expense accounts you usually turn in. You can cut down…"

I closed the door behind me, cutting off the rest of what she was saying.

2

I went to a car rental agency, signed up for a convertible, put the top down, and drove to Colinda.

I cruised around the Miramar Apartments until I had spotted Doris Ashley's automobile. Then I found a parking place, and settled down to wait.

About two-thirty a vivid brunette, who walked impatiently as though her good-looking legs were trying to push the sidewalk out of the way, came bustling out of the apartment house and climbed into the car.

I followed her to the Colinda Supermarket.

I was playing it by ear, without any prearranged plan.

I had to make a pickup but didn't know just how to go about it. The old gag of letting my shopping car swerve and lock a wheel with hers might work. It depended on her mood. But even if it worked, when she got to thinking back on it, she'd find lots of things fishy about my approach. I couldn't afford that.

As someone has said, there are a million approaches you can use to get acquainted with a good-looking girl but none of them is any good unless the girl happens to be in the mood.

The parking spaces near the market entrance were well filled. Most of the vacant spaces were at the extreme end of the parking lot. Doris drove slowly, looking the situation over, then drove to the very end of the parking lot and parked her car up against a wall on the right-hand side. She opened the door on the left and slid out, giving me a flashing glimpse of nylon and leg.

She slammed the car door behind her without even looking

back and walked with her short, quick steps into the supermarket.

There was a vacancy on the left and I parked my car so close to hers that she couldn't possibly open the left-hand door. She was close enough to the wall on the right so she couldn't open that door.

A tall, rangy man parked a Ford sedan next to my car.

I took the keys out of my car, put them in my pocket, went over to a shady place by the corner of the market and waited.

I didn't have long to wait.

Doris came out carrying a brown paper bag filled with groceries. She hurried over toward the place where she had left her car, started to insinuate herself between my convertible and her car, then saw the predicament she was in, hesitated, walked around to the right-hand side and tried to get in there, only to find that the wide door wouldn't open far enough to let her get in.

She looked around, frowning. I could see she was good and mad.

She set the bag of groceries down, walked over to my convertible, looked it over, then reached across to the steering wheel and sounded the horn.

I waited a few minutes, then came sauntering along as though looking for someone, did a double-take when I saw Doris, and turned my head away.

"Is this your car?" she snapped.

"No, ma'am," I said.

She frowned.

"Why?" I asked. "Is something wrong?"

"Is something wrong!" she stormed. "Look at the way this moron has parked. I can't get my car door open and I'm in a hurry."

"Well, what do you know," I said.

She looked me over and said, "What do *I* know? I'll tell you what *I* know. I know what I think of the man who parked that car. I can tell you a lot of things I know about him, but you probably wouldn't think I know the words. Is there any way we can move that damned car? Can we push it back?"

I said, "He's probably in the market. We might be able to find him."

"Sure, we might. We could go in there and page him over the loudspeaker," she said. "I don't want to do it. There are lots of people in that market. I…I'd like to let the air out of his tires."

I said, "I *could* move it if…"

"If what?" she asked.

"I'd hate to get caught," I said.

"Doing what?"

"Short-circuiting the ignition."

She looked me over from head to foot and said, "How long would it take?"

"About ten seconds."

She turned on the charm. "Well?" she asked. "What's holding you back?"

I said, "If I should get caught…I'd go back—"

She showed red lips, pearly teeth, and blinked her big black eyes at me. "Please," she said. "Pretty please!"

I went over to the car, looked furtively over my shoulder, jumped in behind the wheel, took out my knife, scraped insulation from two of the wires, took a short piece of wire from my pocket, jumped the switch, started the car, backed it out and smiled at her. "This all right, lady?" I asked.

She opened her car door, put in the bag of groceries, hesitated a moment, then deliberately elevated her short, tight skirt as she slid in, giving me lots of scenery.

She started her motor, backed her car.

I moved the rented car back up into the position it had previously occupied, opened the left-hand door and got out. She
beckoned me over.

"What's your name?" she asked.

"Donald," I said.

She smiled seductively. "I'm Doris," she said, "and you're a
dear, Donald. How did you learn how to do that?"

"I learned in a hard school, lady," I said.

"Doris," she corrected.

"Doris," I said.

"And you took a chance and did that for me?"

"Yes."

"You're a dear," she said once more, and gave me the benefit
of her smile. "What are you doing here, Donald? You're not
shopping. Are you waiting for someone? Your wife in there
shopping?"

"I don't have a wife."

"Girlfriend?"

"I don't have a girlfriend."

"Why not, Donald?"

"I haven't had the chance to make any contacts—yet."

"What's been holding you back?"

"Circumstances over which I have no control."

"Donald, I might be able to help you. Tell me, what are you
doing hanging around here?"

I let her see that I was hesitating, then finally I said, "It's one
of the checkers. I want to talk with him but I don't want to talk
with him when anyone's around and—they're busy in there."

"They'll be busy in there for a while," she said. "Why don't
you see him when he gets off work?"

"I guess I'll have to."

Her eyes were pools of invitation. "Want a ride uptown?"

"Gosh...thanks."

I walked around the car, opened the door and got in. She made a token gesture of pulling her skirt down with thumb and forefinger, moving it perhaps a sixteenth of an inch.

"I'm going to the Miramar Apartments," she said. "Is that where you'd like to go?"

"Where are the Miramar Apartments?" I asked.

"Three-fourteen Chestnut."

"I guess so," I said. "It's all right with me. That is, one place is just like another."

She backed the car, spun the wheel, made a boulevard stop at the main street, swung out into traffic, flashed me a glance and said, "Look, Donald, you're down on your luck. Right?"

"Right."

"How did you know how to jump-wire that car?"

"Oh, I just knew," I said.

"Have you ever done that before?"

I kept my eyes on the floorboards of the car. "No."

"You don't have to lie to me, Donald. You had that short piece of wire in your pocket. You were hanging around that parking lot. Now tell me why."

I hung my head.

"Donald, tell me. Have you ever been in trouble?"

"No."

"That checker in there you wanted to see, had you known him somewhere? Perhaps in some institution?"

"No."

"Donald, you've been around, you know that you could have got in serious trouble if the owner of that car had come out and caught you jumping those wires. You'd have been in a serious predicament. You know that, don't you?"

I nodded.

"All right. Why take that chance?"

"Because you—you smiled."

"Do my smiles do that to you, Donald?"

"Your smiles, your figure, and your legs," I said.

"Donald!"

I looked back over my shoulder. The tall, gangling guy in the Ford sedan was two cars behind us.

I suddenly fumbled at the car door. "If you wouldn't mind stopping," I said, "I'd better get out here, lady."

"The name is Doris," she said.

"I'd better get out here, Doris."

"I'm going to the Miramar Apartments, Donald. That's where I live."

A signal light turned against us. She pressed a delicate, high-arched foot on the brake pedal. "I *live* there," she repeated.

"Goodbye, Doris," I told her. "You were wonderful."

I opened the door, jumped out and slammed the car door shut.

She started to say something but the light changed and the driver of the car behind her pressed the horn button gently.

She looked at me almost wistfully for a moment, then drove on.

The tall, rangy driver of the Ford sedan was looking for a parking place but couldn't find one. He reluctantly moved on with the string of traffic.

I walked back to the supermarket, fitted my key to the ignition lock and drove back to the city, turned the car in and called Bertha.

"Where are you now?" Bertha asked.

"I'm back in town," I said. "I've been to Colinda."

"Donald, there's something fishy about that case."

"Are you just finding that out?"

"Now, don't be smart. That secretary of yours, Elsie Brand, and those clippings you've been having her save."

"What about them?"

"She's been looking through the personal ads, trying to make a good job of it— My God, the way that girl worships the ground you walk on. What the hell do you do to women, anyway? What are you going to do, marry her? You'd better."

"I will if you insist," I said. "Of course that would make her a partner in the firm."

"Make her what!" Bertha screamed into the telephone.

"A partner in the firm."

"You go to hell. I'm not going to have any goddam secretary marrying into my business."

"All right then, I won't marry her. What did she find out?"

"The insurance company has been running a blind ad."

"What is it?"

"It's an ad offering one hundred dollars for any witness who will testify as to an accident taking place at Seventh and Main Streets in Colinda on August thirteenth, involving a rear-end collision."

"How do you know it's the insurance company?"

"It has to be. Nobody else would have money enough to offer a hundred dollars a witness."

I said, "Why would the insurance company want witnesses? They're going to admit liability. They don't have a leg to stand on as far as the liability is concerned."

"All right, I'm telling you what's in the paper," Bertha said. "You better check in the Colinda paper and see if there's anything in there."

"Good idea," I told her. "I will. I've got some news for you, Bertha."

"What?"

"I've been wearing a tail."

"*You* have."

"That's right."

"Where have you been?"

"Colinda, and back."

"How do you know you're being shadowed?"

"Rear-view mirrors and general observation."

"Donald, what the hell goes on in this case?"

"I don't know," I told her. "Not yet."

"Do you suppose they shadowed Lamont Hawley to our office?"

"I wouldn't know," I said, "but he should."

"Then there's something back of this whole business. You'd better watch your step."

"Oh, no," I told her. "This is one of those nice conservative cases, remember? This is the kind of respectable work that you want us to handle."

"The hell of it is," Bertha yelled into the telephone, "this thing is loaded with dynamite and you know it! Why did that Hawley guy stop in the doorway and tell you there was an element of danger in the case? What the hell was he trying to do?"

"Trying to keep me from running head-on into something I couldn't handle," I said.

"Then why didn't he tell us that when he was briefing us on the case, and tell us what it was?"

I was careful to wait until Bertha had finished talking so my shot would tell, and then said, "Because if he'd been frank with us, you'd have fixed a fee commensurate with the amount of work and danger involved. As it was, he suckered you into fixing a nominal fee. He'd have paid ten thousand just as quick as he'd have paid one, and—"

The inarticulate roar at the other end of the line could only mean one thing.

I gently hung up the telephone before Bertha's screaming indignation could melt the wires in the receiver.

I picked up the agency heap and drove to my apartment, taking it easy and keeping an eye on the rear-view mirror. There was no tail.

I made it a point to get the morning newspapers when they came out late that evening. I looked in the personal ads. Sure enough, there was the ad, but this time they boosted the ante. The ad read: "Will pay $250 for contact with witness who saw rear-end collision Seventh and Main, Colinda, August 13th at 3:30 P.M. Box 694-W."

I clipped out the ad, pasted it on a sheet of paper and scribbled beneath it, call Mayview 6-9423 and ask for Donald.

I addressed the envelope to the box number on the ad and put it in the mail.

Mayview 6-9423 was the number of Elsie Brand's private telephone.

I called her. "Hi, Elsie, how's tricks?"

"Fine, Donald. Where are you?"

"I'm in town."

"Oh, was there something you wanted?"

"Yes, Elsie. If somebody telephones and asks for Donald, be just a little cagey. Tell whoever it is that I'm in and out but that you'll take a message for me. If they want any information or ask for my last name, tell them I'm your brother."

"Are you supposed to be living at this address, Donald?"

"Perhaps."

"Wouldn't it be rather awkward, having a brother living in this single apartment?"

"Okay," I said, "tell them I'm your husband."

"That would be even more embarrassing."

"All right," I said, "which would you prefer, to have it awkward or to have it embarrassing?"

"Which would *you* prefer, Donald?"

"Better leave it just awkward," I said. "Out of consideration for *your* feelings. Tell them I'm your brother."

"Anything you say," she said.

"Sleep tight," I told her, and hung up.

The next day I went to the car rental place and got a Chevrolet sedan. I drove to Colinda.

As nearly as I could find out, no one had the slightest interest in my movements. Aside from normal traffic, I had the road all to myself. I drove fast and I drove slow. I couldn't find anyone following me.

I got to Colinda and bought a newspaper.

There wasn't anything in the want ad column about advertising for a witness who had seen the August 13th accident.

I went to the traffic department at the police station and looked up the records.

There was a routine report that had been made by Carter Jackson Holgate on the day after the accident, mentioning that he had collided with the rear end of a vehicle at Seventh and Main Streets at 3:30 P.M.; that the other car involved was license number TVN 626 and was the property of Vivian Deshler, living at the Miramar Apartments; that damage had been estimated at $150 to the front end of Holgate's automobile; that the damage to the rear of the other car had been "negligible."

I drove out to the Miramar Apartments. Doris Ashley's car was in the parking lot.

A little after two, she emerged from the apartment house and started walking with her characteristic short, snappy stride to the parking lot.

I waited until her back was turned, started my car, drove to the supermarket, parked it and went inside.

Doris entered the market, picked up a shopping cart, made a few purchases and started toward the checker.

I walked up to the checker and lowered my voice. "Look, Buddy," I said, "I'd like to open up a line of credit."

He shook his head. "We're cash."

"But this would only be a short-term credit. I'd just like to have—"

He shook his head again. "I'm sorry," he said. "We just don't have credit, not to anybody. We wouldn't give credit to the President of the United States. We're on a cash basis here. If you want to cash a check, that's something else again. I can refer you to the manager. But no credit."

"Not even for an amount up to five dollars?" I asked.

He shook his head vehemently.

I looked up and saw Doris Ashley standing there staring at me, taking in the whole situation. She couldn't have heard the conversation but she saw the man shaking his head and saw me turning away.

"Donald!" she exclaimed.

"Hello," I said dejectedly.

"Donald, wait for me. Wait, I want to talk with you."

She hurried up to the checking counter, said, "Check these through, please, and give me my change."

She dropped twenty dollars in front of the checker, hurried through and took my arm.

"Donald, why did you duck out on me yesterday?"

"I...I was afraid I was going to go out of control."

"What do you mean, out of control?"

"I said something I hadn't intended to."

"What, about your past? You didn't tell me anything."

"No, about…about your legs."

She laughed. "What about my legs, Donald?"

"They're wonderful."

"Silly boy!" she said. "Did you think I didn't know I had good-looking legs? They're part of me. I use them to walk around with and when I want to impress somebody—well, I *did* give you a good look, Donald, when you were nice to me and had started that car for me."

"You're not angry because I—"

"I'd have been angry if you hadn't."

The checker said, "Here you are, ma'am, three dollars and twelve cents and here's your change out of the twenty."

Doris moved over to the paper bag.

I hesitated for just the right period of time, then said, "May I?" and picked up the bag for her.

I carried it out to the car.

"Just put it in back, Donald."

I put it in back and held the car door open for her. "What are you going to do now, Donald?"

"Going back to San Francisco."

"You saw the person you wanted to see?"

"Yes."

"Get what you wanted?"

"No."

"Get in," she said.

"I—"

"Get in. I'll give you a ride uptown—and don't jump out on me this time."

I got in the car.

Doris had her short skirt up to the hemline of her stockings and this time she didn't make the gesture of pulling it down.

She backed the car out of the stall, drove out of the parking lot and as we left the parking lot I got a glimpse of the tall, rangy individual who had been driving the Ford yesterday. This time he was driving a nondescript Plymouth that had seen plenty of use.

We got into traffic. The Plymouth was four cars behind. Doris said, "Donald, you're lonely, aren't you?"

"Maybe."

"And you've been starved for…for feminine companionship?"

"Could be."

"And you're going to San Francisco, Donald, and you're going to get into trouble. You wanted something here. What did you want—to get a job in that supermarket?"

"Could be."

"And because you couldn't get it, you've given up the idea of going straight. You're going to San Francisco—why?"

"I know somebody there."

"Man or woman?"

"Woman."

"Young?"

"So-so."

"Attractive?"

"Yes."

"You've known her before?"

"Before what?"

"Before you got in trouble."

"Could be."

"Donald, you know what'll happen. You'll need money and you'll meet some of the old gang up there and the first thing you know you'll be in trouble all over again and be back."

"Back where?"

"San Quentin."

She looked at me with a sidelong, searching gaze.

I hung my head and didn't say anything.

"Donald, I want you to do something."

"What?"

"Come up to my apartment."

"Huh?" I said, jolting to quick attention.

"I just want to talk with you," she said. "I want to find out something about you. Perhaps I can help you. Are you hungry?"

"Not too hungry."

"But you're hungry?"

"I could eat."

She said, "Look, I've got a nice filet mignon in the ice box. I'm going to cook that for you and you're going to sit down and relax. You're under some sort of tension and it bothers me. You're too nice to just go drifting back into trouble."

"You're taking an awful lot for granted," I told her.

"People have to take each other for granted sometimes."

I didn't say anything for a while, but watched her driving the car.

"Like them today, Donald?" she asked.

"What?"

"The legs."

"They're wonderful."

She smiled.

We drove in silence until we came to the apartment house. She parked in the vacant lot.

Out of the corner of my eye I saw the tall, rangy guy in the Plymouth park at the curb half a block away.

I got out of the car, walked around and held the door open for her.

She swung her knees from under the steering wheel and slid to the ground. "You can take the bag of groceries, Donald."

"Yes, ma'am," I said.

"Doris," she said.

"Yes, Doris."

I took the bag of groceries and closed the car door. We walked to the apartment house and went up in the elevator.

Doris walked down to her apartment, fitted the key to the door, walked in and said, "Make yourself at home, Donald. Would you like a drink?"

"I don't think I'd better."

"It is a little early," she said. "I'm going to cook you a nice steak."

"No," I said, "you don't have to. I—"

"Hush," she said. "You sit right down in that chair and be comfortable and I'm going to broil that steak and I'll talk with you while the steak's broiling."

I sat in the comfortable chair she indicated.

Doris moved around with swift efficiency.

"You're not going to have much in the line of vegetables," she said, "but you're going to have a darned good steak, with bread and butter and potato chips and coffee....How do you like your steak, rare, medium...?" she hesitated.

"Rare."

"Good," she said.

"You?" I asked her.

"I've just had breakfast, not too long ago—besides, I'm watching my figure."

"So am I," I told her, and then caught myself up short.

She laughed and said, "Go ahead and watch, Donald. I don't mind."

She plugged in a coffee percolator, put the steak in the broiler, and came over and sat on the arm of my chair.

"Are you looking for something to do, Donald?"

"Yes."

"Perhaps you could do something for me."

"What?"

"A job."

"I'd love it."

"It might be—well, a little risky."

"I'd take risks for you."

"Donald, don't keep moving away from me. I'm not going to bite you."

"I'm afraid."

"Afraid of what?"

"Afraid of what I might do."

"What might you do?"

"I don't know."

"Donald, you're lonely. You've been deprived of women for so long you've forgotten how to treat one. Put your arm around my waist. Here…like this."

She took my arm. I put it around her waist.

She smiled down at me.

I tightened my arm.

She slid off the arm of the chair and into my lap and her arm was around my neck. Her lips were pressing against mine. Then her mouth opened slowly and she melted into my arms.

After a minute she said, "Donald, you're wonderful. Now be a good boy for a few minutes. I've got to watch that steak."

She slid down off my lap and went to the broiler, took a long-handled fork, turned the steak over, put the fork down and was starting back to the chair, her eyes starry, her lips parted, when the buzzer sounded on the door.

For a moment her eyes were startled and incredulous. Then she half-whispered, "No, oh, no!"

The buzzer sounded again.

Doris came running to me. She grabbed my hand, pulled me up out of the chair. "Quick, Donald," she whispered. "In this closet. In there. Stay there. It'll only be a few minutes. Quick!"

I showed apprehension. "Your husband?" I asked.

"No, no, I'm not married, silly. It's— Quick, in here."

She led me to a door and opened it. It was a long closet, stretching the length of the room, with feminine wearing apparel on one side and a wall bed which swung out on a door on the other side.

I slipped in among the garments and she swung the door closed. Then I heard the door of the apartment open and a man's voice said, "What's cooking?"

She laughed and said, "Coffee."

I heard him come in and close the door. I heard the rustle of motion, then the man's voice saying, "Hey, this chair is warm."

"Of course it's warm," she laughed. "I was sitting there. I'm warm—or didn't you know?"

"I know," he said.

Again there was silence for a minute. Then the voice said, "What you been doing, Doris?"

"Shopping."

"Anything new?"

"Not yet."

"Something's got to break pretty quick."

"Uh-huh."

I could hear her moving around in the kitchenette, then the aroma of coffee. I heard a cup against a saucer.

"Did you notice the ante's gone up?"

"What ante?" she asked.

"For witnesses to the accident. It was a hundred dollars yesterday. Today's paper makes it two hundred and fifty."

"Oh," she said.

There was quite an interval of silence. Then the man said, "You haven't heard anything?"

"No, of course not, Dudd. I'd tell you the minute I had anything new."

There was another interval of silence. Then the man's voice said, "I'm afraid of that damned insurance company. If they keep messing around they're going to upset the applecart."

"And you think they'll keep investigating?"

"If their suspicions once get aroused, they'll investigate until hell freezes over," he said. "We haven't got too much time. You have to milk the cow when the milk's there. When the cow goes dry there isn't any use trying to milk her— What the hell's burning?"

"Burning?"

"Yes. Smells like meat burning."

"Oh, my God," Doris said. I heard her quick steps on the floor, then the man's voice said, "What the hell! What's all this?"

The smell of burning meat permeated even into the closet.

"What the hell are you doing?" the man asked.

"I forgot," she said. "I was cooking a steak. I left it in the broiler and forgot when you came in."

"What were you cooking a steak for?"

"I was hungry."

"What are you trying to pull?"

"Nothing. I was just cooking a steak. My God, haven't I a right to cook a steak in my own apartment?"

I heard steps; heavy, authoritative, belligerent steps. Then a man's voice said, "Okay, Sweetheart, I'll just take a look around. I'll just see for myself what's going on here."

I heard a door open and shut. I heard Doris saying, "Don't,

Dudd, don't," and then the sound of a body crashing against the wall as he evidently pushed her to one side.

Steps approached the closet where I was hiding.

I opened the door and stepped out. The big man who was striding toward the closet came to an abrupt halt.

"You looking for me?" I asked.

"You're damned right I'm looking for you," he said, and started for me.

I stood looking at him, not moving.

Doris said, "Dudd, don't. Dudd, let me explain."

He had his eyes on mine, his lip curled with hatred. I saw the blow coming but didn't try to dodge. The next one would have caught me anyway. I stood there and took it. I felt myself sailing over backwards. The ceiling spun around in a half-circle, something batted the back of my head and I went out like a light.

When I came to there was still the smell of burnt meat all through the apartment. Doris was talking, her voice rapid and frightened. I heard the words from a distance. They registered in my ears but didn't seem to mean anything to my brain. "Can't you understand, Dudd? This is the man we've been looking for. We can use him. I picked him up and was getting acquainted with him. I wanted to make sure about him and then I was going to turn him over to you.

"Now you've gone ahead and spoiled things."

"Who is he?" Dudd asked gruffly, his voice still suspicious.

"How do I know? His name is Donald and that's all I know. He is fresh out of San Quentin. He came here trying to get a job in the supermarket. One of the checkers there was in prison with him and Donald thought this man could help him, but the fellow wouldn't have anything to do with him. I saw him give Donald the brush-off hard.

"That was when I stepped into the picture and—"

"How do you know he's been in San Quentin?"

"He's done time," she said. "You can tell. He denies it but there's no question about it. He's been in trouble and he hasn't been out very long. He's just starved for decent companionship."

"And what kind of companionship were *you* going to give him?"

"All right. If you want to know, I was going to get him over being lonely."

"I'll bet you were."

"I was going to find out about him and then if everything was on the up and up I was going to tell you about it."

"How do you know he was in San Quentin?"

"The way he got acquainted with me."

"How was that?"

"My car was hemmed in by another car. He short-circuited the wires back of the switch so he could get the car back out of the way. I guess he's a professional car thief. He had a short piece of wire in his pocket so he could jump the current back of the switch."

There was a period of silence, then the man said, "Dammit, don't try doing things alone! I've told you I'm furnishing the brains of this operation. All right, get a Turkish towel soaked in cold water and we'll try and bring the guy to."

Their voices still seemed to be coming from a long way off. It seemed to me they were discussing some subject that had nothing to do with me.

I heard the man's feet, then water dripped on my forehead, then an icy cold towel was put on my face. Someone pulled the zipper on my pants, jerked my pants down, my undershirt up, and I felt the cold, wet towel on my stomach.

My stomach muscles tightened involuntarily. I gasped and opened my eyes.

The big man was bending over me, his expression one of puzzled curiosity. "Okay," he said. "That does it. Get up."

I made a couple of abortive attempts and he reached down, grabbed my shoulders, jerked me to a sitting position, then hooked a big ham of a hand in mine and jerked me to my feet.

He looked me over and abruptly commenced to laugh.

"What's the trouble?" I asked.

"Stick your shirt in your pants and pull up the zipper," he said.

He took the wet towel which had dropped to the floor and threw it across the apartment in the direction of the bathroom. It hit with a soggy thump on the waxed floor, and Doris ran and picked it up, vanished in the bathroom and was back in a moment, to stand looking at me apprehensively. "Are you…are you all right, Donald?"

"I don't know," I said, and tried to grin.

"No hard feelings," the man said. "I'm Dudley Bedford. Who are you?"

"Donald."

"What's your last name?"

"Lam."

"Come again."

"Lam."

"L-a-m-b?" he asked.

"Lam," I said. "L-a-m."

Bedford thought for a moment, then threw back his head and laughed. "I get it now," he said. "You're on the lam, huh?"

"No," I told him, "that's my name."

"Got a driving license?"

"Not yet."

"How long you been out?"

I kept silent.

"Come on," he said, "how long have you been out?"

I let my eyes shift from his. "I haven't been in."

"Okay, okay, have it your own way. Now, what the hell are you doing here?"

"I don't know," I said. "This girl was kind enough to offer me a steak."

"Sit down over here," Bedford said. "I want to talk with you a while."

"I don't want to talk with you. I'm finished. I didn't know she was married."

"She isn't married," Bedford said. "There's enough girl there for you and me and six more just like us. I don't own her and she doesn't own me. I'm working with her. Now, the question is, do you want to work with us?"

"No," I said.

"What do you mean, no?"

"I mean no."

"You don't know what the proposition is yet."

"Of course I know what it is."

"How do you know?"

"You told me."

"What did I say?"

"You asked me if I wanted to work with the two of you and I said no."

"Oh, I see," he said, "smart. Like that, eh?"

"Like that," I said. "I know what I *don't* want."

"Well, what *do* you want?"

"I want a chance to get a respectable job."

"How do you know we weren't offering you a respectable job?"

"You didn't have the right approach."

He said, "All right. I'll try another approach."

"Try it," I invited.

"You know who I am?"

"No. You said your name was Bedford, that's all I know."

"You know how I got in here?"

"You rang the buzzer."

"Smart," he said. "Awful smart. Too damned smart. You could get another sock in the puss."

"I probably could."

He said, "For your information, I happen to be the owner of the car you tampered with yesterday. I saw you getting out of the car and getting into a car with Doris here. It happens that I knew Doris so I came up to find out what the hell she was doing having somebody tamper with my car.

"Now then, Donald Lam, it's your turn. You can talk for a while."

"What...what do you want me to talk about?"

"You can talk about anything you goddam please," Bedford said, "but if I were you, and in your position, I'd start talking about some reason why I shouldn't go to the police and tell them that I saw you tampering with my car; that I found insulation scraped off the wires where someone had jumped the switch. In case you don't know it, although I think you do, it's a crime to be caught tampering with someone else's car.

"Now then, *that's* what *I'd* talk about."

I looked at Doris out of the corner of my eye. She winked. I said, "All right, what was I going to do? Your car was blocking the lady's car so that she couldn't open her door and get the groceries in."

"All right, all you had to do was to go into the market and ask for me. I'd have moved the car."

"There wasn't time for that."

"You must have been in a hell of a hurry."

"She was."

"I don't think I'm going to take that explanation."

"It's the only one there is."

He thought for a while and said, "You know, I *could* use you. You could do a job for me and then we'd be square. How would that be?"

"What kind of a job?"

"Something that would require a little daring, a little tact and a little discretion, and then when you got done you'd be all square with the world and if you did a good job you'd have a hundred dollars in your pocket. How would *that* suit you?"

"That hundred dollars in my pocket would suit me fine," I said, "but I don't think I want the job."

"Why not?"

"It sounds…"

"Sounds what?" he asked, as I hesitated.

"Sounds like something you're afraid to do yourself."

He threw back his head and laughed. "Don't be silly," he said. "I'm not afraid to do any job, but I'm not in a position to do this one."

"What is it?" I asked.

"Now," he said, "you're talking. You're getting cooperative."

He reached in his inside pocket, pulled out a wallet, took out a folded column from a newspaper and handed it to me.

The ad had been circled in red pencil, the ad offering a reward of two hundred and fifty dollars for anyone who was a witness to the accident on August 13th at Seventh and Main Streets in Colinda at 3:30 P.M.

"What about it?" I asked.

He said, "You were a witness to that accident."

"I was?"

"That's right."

I shook my head. "I wasn't anywhere near here. I—"

"Listen," he said, "you do too much talking when you should be listening. Now sit tight and listen. Have you got that straight?"

"All right."

"That's better," he said. "You were here in Colinda. You were walking down the street. You saw the accident. A car, a big Buick, driven by a man who didn't seem to be paying too much attention to traffic conditions, rammed into the car ahead. That was a light sports car, one of these low, racy jobs. It was driven by a babe. You're not sure about the make of the car. The impact caused the babe's head to jerk back violently. You saw that much.

"The babe was all alone in the sports car. She was blond, about twenty-six years old, and you saw her when she got out of the car. She was a good-looking babe, just about the right height and weight, neatly dressed—a good-looking chick.

"She and the man got together and showed each other their driving licenses. You went on. You weren't particularly interested. The accident didn't seem to be serious and they evidently didn't think so, because when you were down the street at the next intersection the two cars drove past you. The Buick had a broken radiator and water was trickling out from it, but the other car didn't seem to be damaged at all, except for a dent in the rear of the body. The girl didn't seem to be hurt."

"What do you mean, '*seem to be*'?"

"She looked and acted perfectly normal."

"Was I walking or riding?"

"You were walking."

"What was I doing in Colinda?"

"What *were* you doing in Colinda?" he asked.

"I…I don't know. I'd have to think it over."

"Start thinking."

Bedford turned to the girl. "You got some writing paper here?"

She opened a drawer in a desk and handed him a sheet of stationery.

"Some paste."

"No paste. I have some household cement."

"That's good. Let's try the household cement."

She handed it to him.

He cut the clipping out of the paper, pasted it to the sheet of stationery, said, "Now we're going to have to have an address."

"He can stay at the Perkins Hotel," she said.

"That's good," he said. "Perkins Hotel."

"I'd have to have some expense money," I said.

He nodded casually. "That's easy.…Okay, now write on here as I dictate."

I took the pen he handed me.

"Sit down here at the table."

I sat down at the table.

"Now write, 'My name is Donald Lam. I saw the accident mentioned. You can reach me at the Perkins Hotel.'

"Now sign it, 'Donald Lam.' "

"Now, wait a minute," I said. "Is this going to get me into any trouble?"

"Not if you do *exactly* as I say."

"Then what happens?"

"Then someone gets in touch with you."

"Then what?"

"Then you tell your story."

"That's where they catch me," I said.

"They catch you in that and I'll break every bone in your body," Bedford said.

"Suppose my story doesn't agree with the facts?"

He grinned and said, "The facts will agree with your story. I want you to remember what I told you. You saw the man driving the big Buick. He looked a little bit tired. He wasn't paying too much attention to what he was doing. He was in a stream of traffic. He had tried to cut out around the stream of traffic, saw he couldn't make it and had ducked back in, but he was going faster than the traffic ahead.

"There's a signal at Seventh and Main. It changed and the traffic ahead slowed to a stop. This man was a little behind time with his reactions and he smashed into the car ahead.

"Now, that is something you saw particularly. You saw the girl's head snap back under the impact. It went way, way back. You stood and looked for a moment, saw the traffic crawling around the two stalled cars, saw the man get out, saw the girl get out, saw them exchange addresses from their driving licenses, saw the man go and look at the front of his car and assess the damage; there was water trickling from his radiator. Then he got back in his car; the girl got back in her car. You started on walking."

"Where was I standing?" I asked. "They'll want to know the exact spot."

"Come on," he said. "I'm showing you the exact spot. Sign your name on this statement."

"How about mailing it?" I asked.

"I'll attend to all that," he said. "Come on now, we'll walk down the street and I'll show you exactly where you were standing and exactly where the accident took place.

"Then we'll go to the Perkins Hotel. I'll get a room with a bath....You got any clothes?"

"No."

"All right," he said. "You can get a razor, a toothbrush and what clean clothes you need. You stay in the room."

"How long?"

"Until I tell you to leave."

"I can go out to eat and—"

"Oh, hell yes," he said. "You can go out to eat. You can go out and wander around. You can come and see Doris if you want to, but you keep in touch with the hotel. Every hour or so you check back in to see if there's been a telephone call for you."

"And when a telephone call does come?"

"You saw the accident."

"Who do I tell that to?"

"Anybody that asks."

"And what do I get out of it?"

"You get immunity for tampering with my car," Bedford said. "You get your room at the hotel and here's some expense money."

He pulled a roll of bills from his pocket and handed me a twenty and a ten. "When you get all done," he said, "you get a hundred bucks."

"What about this two hundred and fifty dollars that's mentioned in the ad?"

"That," he said, "you don't get."

"Who does get it?"

"You don't. Now let's quit beating around the bush. I haven't time to be polite. Do you want to take this or do you want me to pick up that phone, call the cops and tell them I've got the man who was tampering with my car yesterday and show them the place in the wires where you scraped the insulation through and jumped the switch?"

"I'll sign the paper," I said.

"That's better," he told me. "Stick your name on there."

I signed the paper.

He folded it and put it in his pocket. "Come on," he said. "I'll show you where you were standing when you saw the accident."

3

Bedford guided me down to Main Street, then walked on until we came to the clock between Seventh and Eighth. He said, "The accident took place at the intersection just ahead."

I paused a moment to look at the intersection.

"No, no," Bedford warned, "take it in your stride. Keep right on walking, Lam. We'll go to the corner, then turn right, cross the corner, then turn left, and keep walking toward Sixth Street. We'll pause to look in a store window at something, then turn around and go back to the corner of Seventh and Main, turn right, then turn left, and walk on down to the Perkins Hotel. That'll give you a chance to see everything.

"Now remember, there were two or three cars ahead of the car that was hit. You can't remember just how many, but you know that the one that was hit wasn't the one that was right up against the intersection traffic signal.

"You'd noticed this car driven by Holgate, although of course you didn't know who he was at the time, but he was evidently impatient and he'd swung out to the left to try and get ahead of the string of traffic. He was making a run for it when something caused him to change his mind. He evidently saw he couldn't make it—you don't know what it was—so Holgate swerved his car back to the right into the line of traffic next to the curb, but he was going pretty fast. The light at the intersection changed to red, the whole string of traffic came to a stop and—"

"As I remember it," I interrupted, "the light changed to amber first. The car that was in the lead could have got through the crossing before the red light came on, but the driver chose to slam on the brakes."

Bedford put a hand on my shoulder and patted me approvingly, as a trainer might pat a smart dog. "Donald," he said, "you're all right! You're a wonder. Now go ahead and tell me what happened after that."

"Well," I said, "everybody had to stop rather fast but this Buick that was driven by a man whose name I now understand was Holgate just didn't stop at all. It kept right on going until it was within maybe three to four feet of the car ahead and then, apparently for the first time, he realized the traffic ahead had come to a dead stop. He slammed on the brakes so hard that I heard the rubber scream for just a tenth of a second and then there was the sound of the impact."

"And then what happened?"

"The other cars went on through the crossing but these two cars stopped, and the girl who was in the sports car that had been rammed, got out and kept feeling the back of her neck with her hand. She seemed just a little dazed. She started to walk toward the front of the car, then turned and walked toward the back where Holgate was coming up. They stopped for a minute and exchanged names and addresses from driving licenses, and then the girl got in her car and drove off.

"Holgate walked around to look at the front of his car, which was leaking water from a punctured radiator, shook his head, got in his car, seemed rather surprised when it started to run, and then he drove off.

"The whole episode didn't take over a minute, I guess—not more than the length of time required for a traffic signal to change maybe once, maybe twice."

We reached the corner and waited for the signal.

"That's fine," Dudd said. "Now, if the accident took place

between the third and fourth cars back from the intersection, that would put the car that was struck—"

"Right in front of the theater entrance," I said. "That's the way I remember it."

"And the other car?"

"Well, the other car would naturally have been about fifteen feet farther back, just a car's length."

"You heard the noise of the impact?"

"I heard the noise but there were traffic noises and it was surprisingly quiet for an accident. I suppose that was because it wasn't a head-on collision but one car rammed the tail of another."

"Did it attract a lot of attention?"

"A few people looked but they kept on going about their business."

"What did you do?"

"Well, I stopped until I saw the man getting ready to drive away."

"Why?"

"Why did he drive away?"

"No, why did you stop?"

"I don't know, just natural curiosity, I guess. And the girl was most attractive. I wondered if she was all right because I saw her head shoot back when the car hit. Evidently her neck was relaxed at the time because her head just snapped back."

We crossed the street to the right. Dudley Bedford said, "Hell, Lam, you don't need to walk around the corner with me. Start back on this side of the street. Stop when you get to the theater and we'll look to see what's playing."

I walked across the street with him, then we turned to the right and started back down on the other side of Main Street. We paused at the entrance to the movie theater, looked at the announcements of what was playing, and Bedford said in a quiet voice, "You've got the scene of the accident all fixed?"

"Sure," I told him. "I saw it. It was the afternoon of August thirteenth—about three-thirty."

Again he clapped me on the back. "Donald," he said, "you're a regular guy! All right, we'll walk down here to the Perkins Hotel, that's a block and a half. It's about the best we have in this town....Now, you'll be getting a call inside of an hour so be available."

"And after that?" I asked.

"After you get the call," he said, "you'll want to go talk with this man."

"Who'll be calling? Some insurance company?" I asked innocently. "Or an attorney, or—"

"No," Bedford said, "you may as well know it now as later. The man who is going to call you will be Carter J. Holgate. He's a real-estate subdivider and he has a partner by the name of Chris Maxton. They have lots of irons in the fire. Holgate and Maxton."

"Why," I said, "I've seen their name a lot. It's—"

"Sure. They're subdividers," Bedford said. "There's one of their trucks now. They carry their own lumber, buy it in carload lots."

I watched as the big truck with the name painted on the side, HOLGATE & MAXTON, rumbled on past.

"They have activities near here?"

"Right now they're putting on a subdivision about three miles out of Colinda," Bedford said, putting his hand on my elbow and gently guiding me down the street. "We don't want to be seen loafing around here, Donald," he explained.

I walked along with him, taking about a step and a half to his one.

"I'm sorry about that sock in the puss," he said. "I lost my temper."

"Forget it."

"I hope I didn't hit you too hard."

"Not *too* hard," I said. "I guess I was out for fifteen or twenty minutes."

"Hell, you weren't out for more than a minute and a half or two minutes," Bedford said, "but I sure am sorry about it."

"That's all right."

"I'll make it up to you some way."

"Forget it."

"Now about Doris. I lost my temper but that doesn't mean I'm building a fence around her. I want you and Doris to be friends. You're lonely and—well, you just go ahead as soon as you get this chore done. You see all you want of Doris. I'm probably going to be out of town for a few days."

"How long do I stay at the Perkins Hotel?"

"You stay there until you get a call from Holgate."

"And then what?"

"Then go out and see him. Talk with him. Tell him about the accident."

"Is he the one who offered the reward for the witness?"

"Now look, Donald, you're asking lots of questions. You're not supposed to ask questions. You're supposed to tell the facts."

"Okay," I said.

"Then you can stay at the hotel tonight and tomorrow— Well, why don't you run out and see Doris? She likes you and she's a good kid. She'll tell you what I want you to do after that—mainly I want you to keep in touch with me—and of course I'm not loaded with dough; but we'll try and see if we can't get you something that you can do."

"That'll be just dandy," I told him.

We walked on down the street until we came to the Perkins Hotel.

Bedford handed me a hundred dollars. "All right, Lam," he said, "you're on your own. This is some more expense money. You get a hundred more when you finish up. I like you."

He gave me another pat on the back and swung off down the street.

The hotel clerk looked me over appraisingly. I said, "Good afternoon. My name's Lam. I came up here on a business deal and it's taking longer than I anticipated. In fact, I can't even see my man for a little while. I want a good room with bath. I want to be sure I get any telephone calls that come in, and I haven't any baggage."

I pulled some bills out of my pocket.

"Quite all right, Mr. Lam," he said after a moment's thoughtful appraisal. "Just sign the register here, please."

We had an affiliate in San Francisco with whom we exchanged courtesies, so I wrote my name and gave the address of the San Francisco agency. I was shown up to a room, tipped the bellboy, took off my shoes, stretched out on the bed and relaxed.

Within an hour the phone rang.

I answered it.

A man's voice said, "Mr. Lam?"

"That's right."

"I'm Carter Holgate of Holgate and Maxton."

"Oh, yes, Mr. Holgate."

"I understand you saw an accident at Seventh and Main Streets on the afternoon of August thirteenth."

"Why, that's right, Mr. Holgate. I did, yes, but I don't know how you found out about—"

"I'd like to talk with you."

"Well, I'll be here—"

"Look, Mr. Lam, I can't get away at the present time, but I'll send a car in for you. You can come out here for a few minutes and then I'll deliver you back to your hotel. How's that?"

"That'll be fine," I said.

"All right. A car will be there within twenty minutes, perhaps fifteen."

"I'll be waiting in the lobby," I said. "Can you describe the man who'll be driving it?"

"It won't be a man, it'll be a woman, my secretary," Holgate said. "Her name's Lorraine Robbins. She's a redhead about... well, I'd better not say anything about age because she's sitting across the desk from me."

I looked at my watch and said, "In exactly fifteen minutes I'll be standing in front of the door of the hotel on Main Street. I'll stay there until she comes."

"That's fine," he said. "Remember the name. Lorraine Robbins."

"I'll remember."

I freshened up, waited ten minutes, took the elevator down to the lobby, nodded to the clerk, walked out and started briskly down the street. Then, when it had registered in the clerk's mind that I was going somewhere in a hurry, I turned and sauntered back to stand by the door of the hotel, just to one side of the revolving door so that the clerk couldn't see me.

She came within the next two minutes, driving a big, shiny Cadillac which she handled as though it had been a baby buggy.

She swung it into the curb with a deft flick of the wrist and the aid of power steering. She braked to a stop, slid across the seat, opened the door and then paused as she saw me standing there.

She was a dish.

Poised there on the edge of the seat, just ready to get out, her skirt well up, her face alert and intelligent, she caught my eye, smiled and moved over as I crossed the sidewalk to the car.

"Well. What a show!" she said. "These modern skirts just won't behave in these low cars....Now, wait a minute. We'd better get things straight first. You're Donald Lam?"

"I'm Donald Lam."

"I'm Lorraine Robbins. If you're ready, let's go."

"I'm ready," I said, sliding into the car and pulling the door shut.

She gave a quick glance to the rearview mirror, put the signal light on a left turn, gave one second glance to make sure, shot out to the left and into traffic.

She threaded her way through the afternoon traffic and across the Seventh Street intersection. "Live here?" she asked.

"Not permanently," I said. "I'm here back and forth."

"So you saw the accident?"

"That's right."

She said, "Mr. Holgate is going to want me to take down what you say in shorthand."

"Now?" I asked.

"Heavens, no. I'm driving the car now. Later on, when you talk with him."

"Okay by me."

"What do you do, Mr. Lam?"

"Almost anything," I said.

She laughed and said, "I didn't mean it that way. I mean what's your occupation?"

"I'm sort of between jobs at the moment."

"Oh."

She flicked the directional signal over to right, glided around a right turn on First Street, then speeded up.

She handled the car with such skill that she never seemed to have to use the brakes, simply picking the potential openings in traffic before the opening itself had materialized. Then, by the time she got there, the opening had developed and she was able to glide through with a touch of the throttle.

It was a swell job of driving.

"You're Mr. Holgate's secretary?"

"His, and Mr. Maxton's. It's a partnership. Real estate, sub-divisions."

"Lots of correspondence?" I asked.

"Correspondence," she said, "telephone calls, contracts, options, receipts, figuring interest, keeping a tickler system for time payments, running errands, making a sales pitch once in a while."

"How big's the subdivision here?" I asked.

"Quite a project," she said. "Right at the moment it's taking just about full time for everyone, but that's the way things go in this business. You're working at high speed to full capacity one day and the next you're carrying a fifty percent overload and the next you're working twice as hard—and I like it."

"You seem to be good at it."

She flashed me a glance and said, "I try to be good at every-thing I do. I think a girl owes that much to herself—and to her employers. This is a competitive world. You can't get anywhere if you aren't good. If you're going to do anything, do it so you make an outstanding performance. That's my motto."

"It's a pretty good philosophy," I told her.

"Thanks," she said. "I like it."

She swung the wheel to the left, then to the right into a semicircular driveway, came to a stop in front of a typical real estate subdivision building and said, "Here we are."

A big sign said HOLGATE & MAXTON, SUBDIVIDERS and

then underneath in large red letters outlined with a green border: BREEZEMORE TERRACE ESTATES.

I got out of the car and stood for a moment, ostensibly taking in the surroundings with an air of deep approval. Actually I was looking around to see if there was any sign of the person who had been shadowing me.

I couldn't see anyone.

Down at the place marked *Parking* there were half a dozen cars and in a couple of places salesmen were showing potential customers blueprints of the subdivision. A couple of hundred yards farther up the hill I could see three or four parties standing on the curving driveways inspecting lots.

The real estate office consisted of typical freakish high-peaked portable structures which had evidently been trucked out to the location separately and then joined together.

Lorraine Robbins got out of the car on the left, walked around to where I was standing, said, "What do you think of it?"

"Sure looks good," I said. "It's a beautiful site."

"The best suburban homesite in the country," she said. "It's a shame somebody didn't open this up sooner because there's a tremendous population pressure in this area. Believe it or not, the horny-handed son of toil who owned this place had been operating it for fifty years as a dairy."

"You mean no one approached him to—"

"Sure, they approached him," she said, "but he wouldn't listen. He'd got this place as a dairy and, by gum, it was going to keep right on being a dairy! Gosh all tarnation, what do you think I am, anyway?"

Lorraine's flexible voice changed so that she gave a perfect mimicry of an obstinate old man.

"So," I said, "he died."

"He died, and when the heirs saw the appraisal of the land

on the basis of inheritance tax, they fell all over themselves getting in touch with Holgate and Maxton. Actually they got in touch with three different subdividers. We made them the best offer.

"Want to go in?"

"It's so beautiful out here that—"

"Mr. Holgate is expecting you. He's held his time open."

I grinned at her and said, "Let's go."

She led the way into a reception room where the walls were plastered with photographs and maps. There were half a dozen desks in here and at three of the desks salesmen were evidently closing deals, giving receipts and taking checks.

To the right was an office door with a sign, CHRISTOPHER MAXTON, and to the left one that said, CARTER J. HOLGATE.

The back part of the reception room had three typewriter desks, some telephones and filing cases. A good-looking brunette was hammering away on a typewriter. "My assistant," Lorraine said over her shoulder as we turned toward Holgate's office.

The assistant looked up with big, romantic dark eyes and smiled directly at us, vivid red lips parting over pearly teeth.

She got up and came toward us.

She was a long-legged, graceful, statuesque girl who could have won first prize in a bathing-beauty contest hands down.

She said, "Is this—"

Lorraine cut her off. "For Mr. Holgate," she said. "We're going in."

She opened the door without knocking and left the brunette standing there looking at me, the smile on her face but her eyes no longer smiling.

Holgate's office was a big sumptuous room with a long table containing model dwellings, built to scale and placed on lots on a papier-mâché sloping hillside which had been carved with contour roads, covered with green paint to simulate lawns, and had artificial trees growing here and there. The scale houses were on the level lots and could be moved from lot to lot. Their red tile roofs gleamed in artificial sunlight thrown down by a powerful searchlight in the ceiling.

Holgate's desk was a huge affair covered with various knick-knacks and a few loose papers.

Holgate himself, in his late forties, a big, beaming individual with shrewd gray eyes, a slight drawl and the easy affability of a successful salesman, got up to shake hands.

The guy looked like a tall Texan. He was wearing Pendletons and cowboy boots. He must have been well over six feet two and he had the kind of face that would break into a smile at the slightest excuse.

"How are you, Mr. Lam, how are you? It's certainly nice of you to come out. Please sit down there." He had a close-clipped iron-gray mustache which gave strength to his mouth.

I shook hands and told him I was glad to have an opportunity to meet him, that he had a nice-looking subdivision and it looked as though it was headed for a big success.

"Of course it is, of course it is," Holgate said. "We have some of the finest homesites anywhere in this part of the country but we've got something more than that, Lam. We have an opportunity for people to make money.

"We got in on this subdivision right, and we're selling it right. We're splitting the potential profits with our customers.

"I don't mind telling you I'm a fast worker. I get into a place, clean it up and get out. I don't like these subdivisions that drag on and on and maybe a week or two will pass before there's a sale; sometimes a month—not for me. I buy property right and then I split the potential profits with the customers so that I move the whole subdivision within a short time, then make a blanket deal with some financial company to take over what lots are left and go on to something else.

"That way I make a low margin of profit but I have a fast turnover. I— Hell's bells, Lam, I sound like I'm trying to sell you a lot. I'm not—although if you *did* want to put some money into one of these lots it would be the slickest, safest method of doubling, tripling and quadrupling your money you ever saw.

"Well, here I go again, getting too enthusiastic, and talking real estate. I wanted to talk to you about the accident."

"Oh, yes," I said.

"Would you mind telling me just what you saw, Mr. Lam?"

I said, "Well, it was about half-past three o'clock in the afternoon on the thirteenth of August."

Holgate nodded to Lorraine Robbins. She dropped into a chair, whipped a shorthand book off the desk and her pen started flying over the pages.

"If you don't mind," Holgate said, "I'll ask my secretary to take a few notes so that we can keep things straight. There's so much going on around here I try to make notes of everything; otherwise I forget....I don't think my memory is as good as it used to be. How's yours?"

"Seems to be working all right," I told him.

"Well, you're young," he said. "It should be. Now let's see, where were we?"

"Three-thirty on the afternoon of August thirteenth," Lorraine said.

"Oh, yes. Would you care to go on, Mr. Lam?"

I said, "I was walking on the west side of Main Street approaching the intersection of Seventh and Main. Over on the east side where northbound traffic was going I noticed a string of cars. I guess there were probably four or five in the string— well, probably four.

"Now, I was noticing the intersection because I intended to turn to the right and cross over to the east side of Main Street and I was wondering just how it was going to be for catching the traffic signal, so I was watching the light.

"The light changed from green to amber. The car that was nearest the intersection could have gone through all right but the driver slammed on his brakes hard. The car behind him almost hit him. The next car was driven by a young woman— very attractive— Now wait a minute. I think it was the next car. There may have been three between her and the corner but the way I see it now there were only two."

I closed my eyes as though trying to recall the scene.

"Yes, yes, go ahead," Holgate said.

"This car was a light car. I don't know whether it was foreign-made or not. It was a sports car and the top was down. I remember that because I could see this girl when she got hit; that is, when the car got hit. I could see her neck snap back—I mean, her head snap back."

"Yes, yes, go on," Holgate said.

"It was a big car that was behind," I said. "That is, not the biggest but a good-sized automobile, a Buick as I remember, a big one, and—well, that man simply didn't stop in time. He'd been out on the left-hand lane, evidently trying to pass, because when I first noticed him he was swerving back to the right to get in the line of traffic and—"

"Yes, yes, yes," Holgate said. "Now, did you see that man clearly enough to recognize him?"

I shook my head. "Not then."

He frowned slightly.

"Later on after the accident," I said, "I saw him get out of the car."

"You recognized him then?"

"Not at the time because I didn't know him, but I recognize him now. You were that man."

A big smile broke over his face. "And whose fault would you say it was?"

"Lord, there's no question about whose fault it was," I said. "I'm sorry to say this, Mr. Holgate, and I hate to be a witness against you, but it was your fault all the way. You slammed into the rear of the car. That is, I say you *slammed* into it. You started putting on your brakes hard about three or four feet before you got to the rear of the car. That cut down the impact a lot—in fact it was surprising how little noise the accident made. But nevertheless you hit that light car with sufficient force so that—well, I *saw* the girl's head snap back."

"Yes, yes, and then what happened?"

"She got out of the car, you got out of your car, you evidently showed each other your driving licenses and made notes."

"How did the young woman act when she got out of the car?"

"Sort of dazed," I said. "She kept putting her right hand to the back of her neck, and then when you showed her your driving license, and as she made a note of the name, she kept rubbing her neck with her left hand."

"Then what?"

"Then she got in the car and drove away."

"Do you know the exact location of this accident?"

"Sure. It was on the east side of Main Street just before you come to the Seventh Street intersection. It was just about in front of the entrance to that motion picture theater there."

Holgate said, "Lam, I'm going to ask you to do something."

"What?"

"I want an affidavit from you."

"Well, why not?" I asked.

He beamed at the secretary and said, "Draw it up, Lorraine. Use his exact words, make it verbatim."

She nodded, got up and crossed the office.

When she had gone out I said, "There's a remarkable young woman."

"One of the most efficient secretaries I've ever had," Holgate said. "But I have to have efficiency."

"She's also one of the most beautiful," I said. "And her assistant seems to be no slouch either."

Holgate grinned. "Window dressing, Lam. I have to have them beautiful. Did you ever buy a lot in a subdivision?"

"I don't know that I have."

"Well, there has to be a first time sometime, Donald. You'd better buy one in *this* subdivision and really make some money.

"You understand I can't give you any money for your testimony. That would make it worthless. But I could give you the inside track on one of our lots and— How I talk. I can't keep away from making a sales pitch. What were we talking about, Donald?"

"Secretaries."

"Oh yes," he said. "You know, you should see the other one. She's a very wonderful blonde."

"You have three?"

"Lorraine has two assistants. The other one is off today—but what I was going to say was, Donald, that if you ever bought a lot in a subdivision from a salesman and then came in to have the secretaries make out the papers and there was some crabby, hatchet-faced battle-ax on the job, you'd get out of the buying mood.

"I want beauty. Two of those girls won beauty contests. They have what it takes, and I tell them to be friendly, affable. Meet the customer halfway. That's my motto.

"We keep things jazzed up around here. Right from the time the customer arrives on the ground we try to give him a feeling of importance, and we try to get him in the right mood....Take for instance the way these girls get out of a car.

"I don't know whether you've ever seen any of these motion pictures or not, showing young women the modest way to get out of a car; refined, ladylike—to hell with that stuff! When they get out of a car here we just reverse the process. We give them a motion picture lesson of how to get out—that is, if they're dealing with a man. If they're dealing with a woman, of course, the situation is different."

"And when it's a couple?" I asked.

"When it's a couple they have to use their own judgment, find out who's wearing the pants in the family, who's going to sign on the dotted line.

"You know, it's a funny thing about men, Donald. They go down to the beach and they see a girl's legs just as far as there are any legs and they look, but it's just a look.

"But when they see a girl getting out of an automobile, if it looks accidental, if she just gives them a brief glimpse—you know, just a flash—about half as far as they'd see in a bathing suit but— Boy, it makes a man feel devilish. He thinks he's seen something.

"Now, you take women. Just look at the psychology of the thing. When they've got on stockings and a skirt, if you see their legs above the top of the stocking, they act like you're a Peeping Tom—and as far as panties are concerned, my God, that's sacred ground.

"But you let that skirt be labeled a play skirt and the panties made of the same material as the skirt and what happens? They act like it's perfectly all right to whip the skirt off and parade around in panties, just because the panties are made of the same cloth as the skirt. I don't get it. It's a kind of feminine psychology that— But what the hell, I use it, Donald. I use everything. I use all kinds of psychology in sales. Well, here we are…"

He broke off as the door opened and Lorraine Robbins came back in and handed me two sheets of paper and gave a copy to Holgate.

The typing was letter-perfect; neat, even, regular typing with the new modern electric typewriter. It looked as though it had been done on a printing press. There wasn't an erasure, there wasn't a strike-over, there wasn't the faintest irregularity.

And the thing was a verbatim transcription of what I had said.

"Any objection to signing it?" Holgate asked.

"None whatever," I told him.

He handed me a fountain pen.

I signed on the dotted line.

"Any objection to swearing?" he asked. "Just to make it official."

"None whatever."

He glanced at Lorraine Robbins. Lorraine said, "Hold up your right hand, Mr. Lam."

I held up my right hand.

"You solemnly swear that the statements contained in this affidavit which you have just signed are true, so help you God?"

"I do."

She had been carrying a notarial seal concealed in her left hand, one of these little pocket nickel-plated doodads that a notary public can slip into a purse when she's going out.

She pulled the document over to her and on the place where it was written: "Subscribed and sworn to before me this 5th day of October," she signed her name as notary public, impressed the seal and handed it to Holgate.

Holgate looked at it, nodded, got up and gave me his hand, signifying that the interview was over.

"Thank you, thank you very much, Lam. It's wonderful to have citizens come forward and volunteer information in regard to accidents they've seen.

"Now Lorraine will take you back to your hotel—unless you want to look over some of our lots. If you do, she'll be glad to show you around and—"

"Some other time," I said. "I'm—well, I'm not in a position where I care to make any investments at the moment. I don't have any surplus capital to tie up."

His tongue made clucking sounds of sympathy. "Too bad, too bad," he said. "That's the way it is, though. So many times when you have an opportunity for an absolute surefire profit you can't put your hands on the available money. We'll take a small down payment, Lam, and…"

I shook my head firmly.

"Okay, okay. I'm not going to press you. I just feel sufficiently grateful to put some profit your way—you know, something I could do legitimately. Lorraine, take him up to the hotel.… Now, wait a minute, Donald. I don't think your address is in the affidavit."

"It's on the hotel register," I said.

"Well, you'd better let me have it so I can make a note right on this affidavit. Where can I reach you?"

I gave him the San Francisco address.

He came around the desk, put a big hand on my left shoulder, grabbed my right hand and shook it. "Thank you, Donald. Thanks a lot. Any time you want anything in the line of real estate, you just let me know. I'll tell you what I'm going to do. I'm not going to tell you what lot it is because that wouldn't be fair, but I'm going to take one of our best lots and sort of hold it back so that in case you want to get in on the ground floor any time within…well, within the next thirty days, just let me know."

"Now, let's not have any misunderstanding, Mr. Holgate," I said. "That accident was your fault."

"I know it was. I'm responsible," he said. "I'm to blame. I only hope that poor girl isn't injured seriously."

"So do I," I said. "She's a good-looking girl."

"You notice those things, don't you, Donald?"

I looked at Lorraine and said, "I notice those things."

He laughed and said, "Take him to the hotel, Lorraine."

She smiled at me and said, "Ready, Mr. Lam?"

"Ready," I told her.

We went out to the car. I started to walk around to the left side to help her in but she jerked the door open on the right side, jumped in and slid across the seat.

I got in beside her, shut the door and she touched a shapely toe to the throttle and we swept around to the driveway.

"How did you like Mr. Holgate?" she asked.

"Fine."

"He's a wonderful man. A fine man to work for."

"How about Mr. Maxton?" I asked.

The half-second of silence could have been due to the fact that she was concentrating on approaching the intersection. It could have been due to something else.

"*He's* fine," she said.

"You must have a nice job."

"I do have."

"You like it?"

"I love it."

"You like lots of action yourself?"

"Action," she said, "is life. Inactivity is death. Routine is deadly. I want variety. I want new circumstances arising every minute of every day where I have to use my individuality, my initiative, and what brains I have."

"I think you do all right," I said.

"Thank you, Donald. Has anybody ever told you you're awfully nice?"

"Holgate did," I said, "but I think he wanted to sell me a lot."

She burst out laughing and said, "Donald, you do say the damnedest things! How long are you going to be in town?"

"I don't know."

"Know anyone here?"

"Just a few people."

"Men or women?"

"Both."

"Well," she said, "don't get lonely."

"I won't," I said.

"I'm satisfied you wouldn't," she said, glancing at me, "but in case you do—well, you could always get in touch with me. My name's in the phone directory."

"Would you try to sell me a lot?" I asked.

She laughed again and said, "Probably."

She was silent for two or three minutes, then as she drove up in front of the hotel she smiled at me and said, "And, on the other hand, Donald, I might *give* you a lot."

She gave me her hand with a quick, impulsive gesture, flashed me a quick smile, then turned her attention to the front of the car, waiting for me to close the door.

I closed the door, she gave a quick look into the side mirror and shot out into traffic.

4

The hotel clerk told me there were no messages for me. I told him I'd look the town over a bit and walked a couple of blocks to a taxi stand.

The taxi took me to the supermarket. I got in the car I had left parked there, drove back to the hotel and hung around until dark.

No one seemed to be taking the slightest interest in me. The rangy individual didn't put in an appearance. Nobody seemed to care whether I came or went. There were no messages.

Shortly before dark I called the apartment of Doris Ashley.

There was no answer.

I went to a phone booth and called Elsie Brand at her apartment.

"Hello, Elsie," I said. "How're you coming?"

"Donald!"

"What's the trouble, kid?"

"Some man has been telephoning and he sounds—well, dangerous."

"It's easy to *sound* dangerous," I said. "What does he want?"

"It's about an accident that you saw and he seems to be very —well, he's a little annoyed about things."

"Is that so?" I said. "How often has he called?"

"He's called three times within the last hour. Heavens, I didn't know what to tell him. I told him that I wasn't aware that anyone from my apartment had given him a telephone number but that my brother was visiting me and I expected him in shortly."

"I'll be in shortly," I told her. "Sit tight."

"Donald, is this anything—well, dangerous?"

"How should I know?"

"I'm frightened."

"You don't need to be. I'll be in."

"How soon?"

"Within an hour."

"Oh, Donald, I— You'll be careful, won't you?"

"That's strange," I said. "Usually you tell me to be good. Now you tell me to be careful."

Her laugh was nervous. "Do you want me to cook dinner for you?"

"Might be a good idea," I said. "That would give the place a homey atmosphere."

"What do you want?"

"Champagne and filet mignon," I said.

"I'm a working girl."

"This," I said, "is on an expense account."

"Champagne and filet mignon it is," she said. "You want them thick?"

"Thick."

"Rare?"

"Rare."

"Potatoes?"

"Baked. Don't go to any trouble. Don't try to make a salad or dessert. We're just going to have steak, baked potato, champagne and perhaps a can of green peas. I'll cook the steaks when I get there. When this bird calls again, try to get his name. Tell him that I've been detained but that I phoned you I was coming home in an hour and that we'll be having dinner at that time. Tell him to come in about an hour and a half from now and I can talk with him."

"You be sure to get here before he arrives, Donald."

"I'll be there," I told her. "You buy the steaks and the champagne. Be sure to keep the bills so I'll have a voucher for Bertha."

"Bertha," she announced, "will have kittens all over the lot."

"Do her good," I said. "Sit tight. I'm on my way."

I hung up the phone, hit a little better traffic conditions than I had anticipated and was there within forty-five minutes.

Elsie had the champagne on ice and a couple of thick filet mignons all ready to go in the broiler. There were potatoes baking in the oven and a can of green peas. She also had a loaf of sourdough French bread split and buttered and ready to go in the oven. There was a jar of garlic paste to put on the bread as it toasted.

"Well, this is just like home," I said.

She started to say something, caught herself, then blushed a fiery red, evidently at what she had been about to say.

"You got the bills?" I asked her.

She handed them to me.

"Did our man call again?"

"He called within seconds of when I hung up after talking with you."

"You told him to be here?"

"Yes."

"What did he say?"

"Said he'd be here. Said I could tell my brother that this wasn't any laughing matter and to be absolutely positive he was telling the truth."

"What did you tell him?"

"I told him my brother always told the truth, that it ran in the family."

"Good girl," I said. "Well, we'd better make the thing look brotherly."

I took off my coat, unfastened my cuffs, rolled up my shirt sleeves, pulled my necktie down, opened the collar of my shirt and was looking around for something to do when the buzzer sounded.

"Answer the door," I said to Elsie. "Tell him that your brother has just come in and ask the guy his name.

"When you introduce me, try not to give a last name. Simply say, 'This is Donald.' Do you get me?"

"I get you."

"Let's go."

She went to the door.

The thick-set, aggressive-looking individual who stood on the threshold had bushy eyebrows, thick hair just above the ears and very little on top of the head. He wore an expensive suit but the shoes were badly in need of a shine.

"Hello," he said. "Is your brother in— Oh, yes, I see him."

He started in through the door.

Elsie stood in the doorway. "May I have your name, please?"

"Harry Jewett," he said, and pushed past her into the apartment.

"You're the brother?" he asked me.

"I'm the brother," I said, holding the long barbecuing fork with which I had been ready to spear the steaks, "and where I come from people don't come barging into an apartment unless they're invited."

"I'm sorry. I guess I was a little impulsive. I'm— This is important to me."

"Manners are important to me," I said, "and my sister is a lady."

"Who said she wasn't?"

"Your actions intimated as much."

"Now, calm down, Junior," he said. "I want to talk with you."

"I'm not Junior," I told him. "My name's Donald and you get the hell out of that door, stand in the hallway and wait until you're invited in or you don't talk with anybody."

"I thought it would be something like that," he said.

"Like what?"

"You made a play but you don't dare to talk."

"I thought I was talking," I said. "I thought I said something. I told you to get back out in the corridor."

I advanced toward him, holding the fork.

He squared his shoulders, braced himself, then thought better of it, turned, walked back out to the corridor and knocked on the door.

Elsie, who had been standing riveted to the spot, looked toward me for instructions.

Jewett said, "Oh, good evening, madam, I'm Harry Jewett. I'm sorry to bother you at this time of night but it's a matter of some importance to me.

"I believe your brother witnessed an automobile accident about two months ago and I'd like very much to talk with him."

Elsie rode along with the gag. "Why, how do you do, Mr. Jewett?" she said. "I'm Elsie Brand. Won't you come in? My brother's here now. He just came in."

"Thank you. Thank you very much indeed," Jewett said and entered the apartment.

"How's that?" he asked me.

"That," I said, "is better. You're early. I haven't eaten."

"Won't you be seated?" Elsie asked.

"Thank you," he said.

Under the bushy eyebrows his eyes bored into mine. "Would you mind telling me what you saw?" he asked.

I said, "I believe there was a reward mentioned."

"Two hundred and fifty bucks," he said.

"I don't like to give anything away when the other man has put a price tag on it."

"And I don't want to pay out money for something I can't use. You convince me that you saw the accident and you get two hundred and fifty bucks."

"Fair enough," I told him.

"All right, start talking."

I said, "It was about three-thirty in the afternoon. I was in Colinda walking along the main street—I believe that's what they call it, Main Street. I was going north on the left-hand side of the street and was between Eighth and Seventh Streets. In fact, I was approaching the intersection of Seventh Street and was looking up at the traffic signal to see how it was going because I wanted to go over to the east side of Main Street and wanted to time it so I could cross with the signal."

"Go ahead," he said.

"There was a string of cars—I'd guess about four—approaching the signal. The light turned from green to amber, and the car that was in the lead could have made it easily before the signal turned to red, but instead the driver lost his nerve and slammed on his brakes, *hard*. The car came to an almost instantaneous stop.

"The car behind him braked to a stop just in time to keep from hitting him. The third car was a light sports car with the top down. It was driven by a quite good-looking girl. The car behind her was going pretty fast. The driver had evidently swung out to the left to try and get around the string of traffic because—"

"How do you know that?"

"When I saw him he was swerving back to the right again and going pretty fast."

"What happened?"

"That's about it. The man in the back car, which was a big Buick, ran into the girl in the sports car. He hit her a pretty good jolt. Her car was stopped at the time of the impact. In fact, she'd been stopped for a couple of seconds."

"Did she act injured in any way?"

"She didn't act injured except her neck seemed to be hurting her. She kept holding one of her hands against the back of her neck."

"The hell she did."

I said, "She got quite a jolt when the car hit because the blow was unexpected. I saw her head snap back."

"Did she stop?"

"She was stopped before he ever hit her."

"All right. What happened?"

"Well, they both got out and talked for a minute. Then the girl drove on. The man went to the front of his car, took a look at it, shrugged his shoulders, got in and drove off. The radiator had been punctured, I think, because he was leaving a stream of water on the street.

"That's all I saw. I guess I missed one or perhaps two traffic signals standing there looking at them."

"Did you take down the license numbers?"

"No, I didn't."

"Would you know either of these people if you saw them again?"

"Sure. I had a good look at them."

"Describe the man."

"Well, he was a big tall fellow—looked something like a Texan. He was wearing a brown suit and a sport shirt."

"How old?"

"Oh, forty—forty-two or three."

"Tall?"

"All of six foot two. Sort of a good-natured chap. I saw him smiling, despite the fact the front of his car was caved in. He had a close-cropped mustache."

"What time was this?"

"Right around three-thirty, give or take a few minutes either way."

"And the date?"

"The thirteenth of August."

Jewett said, "I'm going to show you a picture. It may or may not mean anything. Of course I know it's a job to recognize a man from a photograph but I want you to try it."

He pulled a billfold from his pocket, took out a photograph of Carter Holgate. It was a fairly good snapshot showing Holgate and Jewett standing side by side at the entrance to the subdivision with the sign: HOLGATE & MAXTON — BREEZEMORE TERRACE ESTATES.

"You recognize either of those people?" he asked.

"Sure," I said. "That's you on the right."

"And the one on the left?"

"That," I said with firm conviction, "is the man who was driving the car that ran into the girl's car."

"You're sure?"

"I'm sure."

Jewett slowly and reluctantly put the wallet back in his pocket. "Where can I reach you?" he asked.

"Through Elsie here. I always keep in touch with her."

"You going to be living here?"

"I don't think so," I said. "She's putting me up for a couple of days. I'm on my way."

"Where to?"

"I'm not sure."

Jewett hesitated for a moment, then extracted two one-hundred-dollar bills and a fifty-dollar bill from his wallet and handed them to me.

"What am I supposed to do now in return for this money?" I asked.

"Not a damned thing," he said. "Just not a single damned thing."

"Should I know the name of the man who's standing next to you in the photograph?"

"Why?"

"So I can tell him I saw the accident."

"Whose fault was it?"

"It was his fault."

"Do you think he'd like to have a witness who could go on the stand and swear it was his fault?"

I fingered the two hundred and fifty dollars and said, "Well, somebody seems anxious to have a witness."

"You've answered the ad," he said. "You've got the two hundred and fifty. Now, forget it."

"What do you mean, forget it?"

"Just like I told you," he said. "Forget it."

He got up out of the chair with the ease of a trained athlete, walked to the door, turned, looked Elsie Brand over from head to foot and said, "Thanks. I'm sorry I bothered you and I'm sorry I was rude. I really *am* sorry."

He walked out and pulled the door shut behind him.

Elsie looked at me. I could see that her knees were rubbery.

"Donald, who was he?"

"I don't know," I said. "The only thing I'm willing to bet is that I can tell you who he wasn't."

"Well, who wasn't he?"

"He wasn't Harry Jewett," I said.

"What makes you think that?"

"The initial on his cuff links was M. He had an M embroidered on his necktie. The photograph showed the two of them standing under a sign of Holgate and Maxton. The big man with him was Holgate. I have an idea this may have been Christopher Maxton."

"Oh," she said.

I handed her the two hundred and fifty dollars.

"Go buy yourself some socks, Elsie."

"Why, Donald— What do you—"

"This is money on the side," I said. "Get yourself some socks."

"But, Donald, you'll have to turn that in."

"Turn it in on what?"

"As a credit."

"As credit for what?"

"For the money that was paid to you—you know, against whatever expenses you're charging."

I shook my head. "This is side pickings, Elsie. Get yourself some nice sheer nylon stockings. Wear them around the office and be as generous as possible."

Her face got red again. "Donald!" she said.

I kept holding out the bills and after a moment she took them.

5

It was 9:45 when I got back to Colinda and found a parking place for my car about a block from the hotel. I walked down the street and turned in at the hotel. I nodded to the night clerk.

"Are you Mr. Lam?" he asked.

"That's right."

"There have been a couple of messages for you. I put them in your key box. Do you want them?"

"Sure."

He handed me two messages. One of them had been received at eight o'clock and said: *Mr. Lam, please call me as soon as you come in. Carter J. Holgate.*

The other one had been clocked at nine-thirty and said: *No matter what time you come in it is absolutely necessary for you to see me. I'll be waiting at the office. This is a matter of the greatest importance. The number is Colinda 6-3292. Be sure to call. Holgate.*

The clerk said, "He seemed most anxious, Mr. Lam. I told him I'd be sure that you received the messages. That last call was only a few minutes ago."

"How did you know who I was?" I asked.

"The day clerk described you to me. He said you were anxious to receive any messages that came, as soon as they were received at the desk."

"Okay, thanks," I told him.

I went up to my room and called the number given by Holgate. It didn't answer.

I called Doris Ashley's number.

It didn't answer.

I went down to the lobby, told the clerk, "Guess I'll go out for a cup of coffee. If any more messages come in, tell them I'll be back in—oh, half an hour or so."

I walked out to my car and drove out to the Breezemore Terrace Estates. It took me about eight minutes.

The right wing of the building containing Chris Maxton's offices were dark. There were lights on in the reception part of the building and lights on in the left wing which contained Holgate's offices.

I parked my car, walked up the steps, entered the reception room and called out, "Yoohoo! Anybody home?"

The place was utterly silent.

There was a sepulchral quality about the silence—the office with all the trappings of modern business, the desks, the electric typewriters, the overhead lights, the filing cases, all silent and deserted. The typewriters all had plastic covers except one from which the plastic cover had been removed and a telltale pilot light over the switch showed that the current was on.

I walked through the swinging gate to the back of the room and took a look at the typewriter. The electric motor was purring away smoothly. I put my hand on the machine. It was warm, indicating the motor had been on for some time.

I walked over to the door of Holgate's private office and knocked.

There was no answer.

I hesitated a moment, then opened the door.

The interior of the office was a holy mess. A chair had been overturned and smashed; the papier-mâché model subdivision had been knocked off the table, all of the beautiful model houses had been scattered over the floor and some of them had evidently been trampled on, as they were broken into bits. The window looking out on the street was open, a faint night breeze was stirring the drapes.

Drawers had been pulled out of the desk, and the filing cabinet had apparently tipped over when the last of the full drawers had been pulled out. Someone must have been hastily searching for something.

A woman's handbag was on the floor with one strap broken and the metal frame bent. A compact was lying open with the two covers flattened and smashed.

Parts of a powder cake were on the floor, and bits of glass from the broken mirror.

I picked up one of the broken pieces of powder cake, smelled it and rubbed my fingers along it. The powder was a pale pink with the scent of carnation.

On the floor, half under the papier-mâché model subdivision, was a woman's shoe.

I put my fingers under the edge of the papier-mâché green subdivision and lifted it so I could free the shoe for an inspection.

It was an alligator leather shoe bearing the trademark of a shoe store in Salt Lake City.

It was a neat, narrow little bit of leather with class written all over it. That shoe had cost plenty and called for a dainty high-arched foot.

I walked over to take a look at the litter of papers on the floor by the filing case.

For the most part the papers that had spilled out of the files onto the floor were in brown paper folders, but many had been either pulled out of the folders and scattered over the floor by someone searching for some particular paper, or when the contents of the file drawers had tumbled out, these papers had fallen from some of the envelopes. These papers proved on inspection to be options, contracts and receipts covering down payments. Nearly all of them were on printed forms.

One piece of paper, however, caught my eye. It was a sheet of flimsy with typing in a purple copying ink.

I knew that type of paper all too well. It was the paper used in many detective agencies for making reports to the client.

I pushed the other pieces of paper aside and pulled out this sheet of flimsy, finding as I did so that two other papers were attached to it.

The report read:

"Following instructions to keep subject under surveillance it was deemed advisable to keep a watch on her car to see when she left her apartment house, inasmuch as there was no practical way of keeping her apartment under surveillance except by stationing a man in the corridor, and this would have defeated purpose of client in asking for surreptitious surveillance.

"Therefore, when it became apparent another person was also keeping watch on this car, client was notified by long-distance telephone and we were instructed to put operative on this new subject in order to ascertain his identity.

"At two-twenty-five subject Doris Ashley left apartment and entered her automobile, driving to supermarket in accordance with routine daily procedure.

"Man who had been keeping her car under surveillance drove to supermarket, parked his car so close to that of subject's she could not get in with groceries. Later on this individual, pretending this was not his car, jumped the switch wiring, apparently as an excuse to get acquainted with subject, and this was successful in that subject invited man to ride with her.

"He rode to a point near Eleventh and Main, then abruptly

left subject's automobile, and our operative was unable to pick him up again until the following day when he was again spotted and followed.

"This man's car on which he had jumped wires, turned out to be a car rented from Continental Drive-Yourself Agency in the city but no information was immediately forthcoming on identity of person renting the car.

"The next day this man again was picked up, tailed to the supermarket. At supermarket he approached one of checkers just as subject was about to pay for groceries. Subject recognized him and seemed glad to see him. At her apparent invitation he got in her car, this time riding back with her all the way to subject's apartment. Again it was ascertained this party was driving a car rented from Continental Drive-Yourself Agency, but this time by pretending car had been involved in an accident, our city office was able to ascertain identity of person renting the car.

"This individual is Donald Lam, and Lam is a partner in the detective agency of COOL & LAM.

"This agency is rather unorthodox in its operations and little can be found out about it since it does not seem to be catering to regular clients but goes in for sharpshooting on cases having unusual angles.

"Donald Lam is locally reported to be highly ingenious and resourceful, exceedingly daring and at times undoubtedly disregards professional ethics in order to obtain some real or fancied advantages for his clients.

"In accordance with instructions we immediately communicated information to client by long-distance telephone as soon as it was obtained.

"At this time Donald Lam was in subject's apartment.

"Upon receipt of information as to the identity of the person

*in question, client instructed us immediately to discontinue
all shadowing operations, to close the case, submit final bill
and take no further action.*

*"In accordance with these instructions operative was
recalled to city office and the case closed.*

"ACE HIGH DETECTIVE AGENCY *per J.C.L., Manager*
"Los Angeles Branch"

I studied that report for a moment, then folded and shoved
it in my coat pocket. I looked around but couldn't find any
jacket or brown paper envelope from which this paper had
spilled.

I noticed a door half open which led to a lavatory. I went to
that door, opened it wide and was about to enter the room
when I heard steps in the outer office.

I ran to the window and looked out. There was a car parked
just behind mine. I couldn't see it too clearly but it was a big
shiny car.

I pushed aside the curtains on the open window, eased
myself over the sill and dropped to the ground. I started
walking toward my car, then thought better of it and sprinted.

I jumped in the car, started the motor and eased into motion
as noiselessly as possible.

Someone yelled.

I could see a man's frame silhouetted against the light in the
room, standing in the open window from which I had made my
departure.

"Hey, you!" he yelled. "Come back here! Stop where you
are!"

I stepped on the throttle.

I had a blurred glimpse of the man climbing through the
window and running across the lawn toward his car. Then I

skidded into a turn at the end of the driveway, hit the paved road and pushed down the foot throttle.

I had gone about half a mile before I picked up the headlights in my rearview mirror.

I gave the car everything it had.

A boulevard stop loomed ahead. I shot through it as fast as the car would go, negotiated a turn with screaming tires, hit a straightaway and my headlights picked up another boulevard stop ahead. This time it was a main thoroughfare. I could see headlights approaching as I came to the white line but I pressed my hand on the horn button and shot through.

There was a brief hundredth of a second when headlights were glaring into my eyes from the left-hand side at a distance of not over thirty feet. Then I squeezed on by and was out in the clear.

That gave me time enough to execute a U-turn, slow the car and come driving sedately back.

I was just at the thoroughfare intersection when the car that had been following me roared across the main thoroughfare, also ignoring the boulevard stop, and shot on past me.

The driver was too busy with what he was doing to notice cars that were coming toward him and he never even slowed down as he shot past. I don't think he ever saw anything except my headlights.

I eased out into the main boulevard and joined the stream of traffic.

I headed on the main road to Los Angeles and as soon as I found a service station that had a telephone booth, called Bertha at her apartment.

Bertha's voice was irascible. "What is it this time?" she asked, "and why the hell don't you make reports and let me know what you're doing? Our client has been wondering if you've discovered anything and I have to pull that old crap about making progress and being too busy at the moment to make a written report."

"All right," I said, "it wasn't crap. I *was* making progress and I *was* too busy to make a report. Now I've got to talk with you."

"What about?"

"About progress."

"I'm in bed."

"Well, get up," I told her. "You shouldn't go to bed this early anyway."

"Dammit to hell, Donald Lam!" she screamed in the telephone. "You know I go to bed early and read myself to sleep. I—"

"Read yourself awake," I told her. "I'll be there in less than half an hour."

6

Bertha Cool opened the door of her apartment as soon as I rang. She had on pajamas and her hair was in curlers. She was mad.

"Now will you tell me what this is all about?" she demanded as I entered the apartment and took a chair. "Why in hell can't you go to the office, tap this stuff out on a typewriter and have it so I can show it to the client in the morning?

"Or, the way that damned secretary of yours looks at you with those puppy-love eyes of hers, she'd probably welcome the opportunity to have you get her out of bed and start dictating. Or you might not have to get—"

I interrupted. "This thing is too hot for anything like that, Bertha."

"What's hot about it?"

"I've been made."

"By whom?"

"The Ace High Detective Agency."

"What the hell are they doing cutting in on our case?"

"They're not cutting in on our case. They've got a case of their own. They were hired to keep Doris Ashley under surveillance and to check on everything she did.

"So when I showed up on the scene and started watching her car, the Ace High operative picked me up and reported to the client, whoever the client was, on long-distance telephone."

"Somebody here?" Bertha Cool asked, her eyes narrowing.

"I said long-distance, Bertha. This is a dial operation now from Colinda. Here, take a look at this."

I handed Bertha the Ace High report.

"Fry me for an oyster!" Bertha said when she had finished reading. "Do you suppose, Donald, that Lamont Hawley had another agency working on the case— How did you get this, Donald?"

I told her what had happened.

"Then Hawley must be double-crossing us."

"How else would the Ace High have been on the job?" I asked.

Bertha Cool's greedy little eyes started snapping. "That's it, Donald," she said. "That's what happened. The sonofabitch got two detective agencies, the Ace High and ours, and played one against the other. The Ace High people had been on the job for several days and hadn't got results, so someone told the Consolidated Interinsurance people about you and how you could handle women and that explains why they terminated the employment of the Ace High people as soon as they found out you had made a personal contact with Doris Ashley."

"Whatever the reason," I told her, "let's have a showdown on this thing. I don't like being played for a sucker. I don't like to have a client give me only part of the facts.

"Let's get Lamont Hawley in the office and hand it to him straight from the shoulder."

Bertha said, "That's the spirit, Donald!"

She suddenly started blinking her eyes. "Wait a minute, Donald. We don't have anything to support our claim except this report of the Ace High people, and of course Hawley is going to want to know how we got hold of that and—"

"Don't tell him how we found out," I said. "Let him wonder."

Bertha thought that over, then suddenly her face wreathed in smiles.

"I'd just like to see that sonofabitch's face, Donald. Here he is, trying to play one detective agency against the other. He's had the Ace High people trying to make a contact. They get no-where. We come in, make a contact first rattle out of the box and then the next thing he knows we find out all about the other detective agency and his instructions to them. That's going to curl his hair!"

"All right," I told Bertha. "Now the question arises, where did that report come from?"

"You told me you got it out of Holgate's office."

"All right, how did Holgate get it?"

"He— Fry me for an oyster!" Bertha said, and lapsed into silence.

"He got it from some woman," I said, "who came to the office. And shortly after that someone got into the office and a general fight started. Holgate and the woman were mixed up in it or else the man who came in and started the fight had a woman with him."

"How do you know?"

I told her about the shoe.

"She'd have gone back and gotten that shoe," Bertha said. "A woman can't walk with high heels on one foot and nothing on the other."

"Perhaps she kicked off the other shoe," I said, "and went in her stocking feet."

"She could have," Bertha said, "if for some reason she felt it was dangerous to go back to get the other shoe. All right, what happened then? There was a fight. Who won?"

"The intruder won."

"How do you know?"

"Because he just about wrecked the office looking for some-thing."

"This report?" Bertha asked.

"This report, hell," I said. "This report was left there and there's a damned good chance this report was taken there by the intruder, whoever he was."

"How do you figure that out?"

I said, "The intruder came to the office. He started talking with Holgate. Then he pulled this report out of his pocket and handed it to Holgate for him to look over. That probably started the fight. The office was pretty well wrecked. This girl was in on it because she hit someone over the head with her purse and bent the frame on the purse, at the same time spilling the contents of the purse to the floor.

"When she left, she left the purse because it was bent and wouldn't close, but took the things she wanted to take with her and probably wrapped them in a towel."

"Why a towel?"

"There was a lavatory off the office and there weren't any towels on the rack, but there was one towel that had been jerked to the floor."

"Well," Bertha said, "they can't tie any of that in with us."

"I don't know," I said. "That's the thing that bothers me."

"Why does it bother you?"

"Because this car drove up while I was there and some man came in the office. He could have been a night watchman. It could have been police. I don't know *who* it was. I jumped out the window and made a getaway. He took after me and I outdrove him to a point where I could double back and throw him off the trail."

"Well, you got away from him."

"Suppose he got the license number of the automobile?" I said. "I'd left the rented automobile and was driving the agency car that's registered in our names."

"What the hell did you do that for?" Bertha asked. "My God, if that man got the license number—"

"I was cutting down on expenses," I said.

Bertha glowered.

I grinned at her.

After a while Bertha said, "Don't we have to report something like that to the police?"

"Something like what?"

"Where a man's office has been broken into and—"

"How do we know it was broken into?" I said. "The office door was open. It's a public place. Probably Holgate invited the person in."

"Well then, the place was wrecked and papers were stolen and—"

"How do we know papers were stolen?" I asked her. "Someone was looking for something in the files and was rather careless in the way he conducted his search. He didn't pull the filing drawers out and put them back, he pulled out one drawer after another and after they were all out the weight of the papers in the open drawers shifted the center of gravity so that the whole filing case toppled over. When it did, the papers spilled out and the person who had been conducting the search pushed the filing cabinet back into an upright position and that was all. How do we know he took anything?"

Bertha thought that over.

"In other words," I said, "we don't *know* any crime has been committed and there's no reason for us to report a crime if there hasn't been any crime."

"You're a brainy little bastard," Bertha said. "I wouldn't dare to skate on that thin ice but if *you* think *you* can get away with it, go to it."

"The point is," I said, "I want to know what happened to Holgate."

"What do you mean?"

"Did he wait until the intruders, whoever they were, had left and—"

"Don't call them intruders," Bertha said. "Call them visitors. I like this idea of yours that it's a public office and that Holgate probably invited them in and tried to sell them a lot."

"All right," I said, "when his visitors departed, did Holgate take off after them or—"

"Sure, he took off after them," Bertha said. "His car was gone. You said that when you drove up there, there weren't any cars at all."

I nodded.

"Well, he didn't walk out to the place," Bertha said. "He had his car there. The visitors left in their car and then Holgate left in his."

"Before or after he called me?" I asked.

"Probably before," Bertha said.

"Let's hope so," I told her.

"You don't think so?"

"I don't know, Bertha. Since they know who I am, this thing may get a little ticklish. I think we should call Lamont Hawley. Do you have a night number where you can reach him?"

"Hell, no," Bertha said. "He didn't give me any night number. This was supposed to be respectable business. He gave me a private number but I don't suppose—"

"My God, Donald, I don't know what it is about you. Every time you start working on a case the damned thing blows up into some kind of an emergency and every now and then there's a corpse."

"Well, let's hope this is the then," I said.

"What do you mean?"

"If it's a corpse now," I told her, "it could be bad business."

Bertha blinked her eyes. "What the hell are you talking about?"

"I'm talking about what would happen if it should turn out there was a corpse."

"Who do you mean?"

"Holgate."

"Don't be silly."

"What's silly about it?"

Again Bertha blinked her eyes. "Dice me for a carrot!" she said.

There was a moment's silence, then Bertha said, "Wait a minute. You're just talking about somebody seeing the license number on your automobile. But what about fingerprints? You went out of there in a hell of a hurry. You must have left—"

"I left fingerprints all over the place," I said. "Don't be silly. I'm going to fix that."

"How? You can't go back and wipe all the fingerprints off. You don't even know all the places where you put your hands."

"Of course not," I told her. "I'm going back and leave more fingerprints."

"How come?"

"That's one of the oldest gags in the book," I told her. "If you can't get rid of your fingerprints at the scene of a crime, make some excuse so you go back when you have a witness with you. Then you touch everything in sight. When the police find a fingerprint there's nothing on it that tells when it was made. The only time element on this one is the powder cake out of the compact. I got that on my fingers and then touched things. I want to be sure to go through that routine again when I'm out there the second time."

"And when's that going to be?"

"Right now," I told her. "Now look, Bertha. Get busy and try and locate Lamont Hawley. The guy has a telephone somewhere, and the insurance company has some kind of an investigative service that has a night number. Get hold of Hawley and tell him what the score is.

"You can keep this report from the Ace High agency. I don't want to have it with me. There's one clue there. Notice that a part of the second page has been torn off, but there's an expense account there with a long-distance bill of a dollar and ninety cents. And the woman's shoe that I found out there was sold in Salt Lake City. So I have an idea you'll find the telephone call was made to Salt Lake City and that's where the client was living. As soon as the Ace High client found out I was a detective, she grabbed a plane and flew on to—"

"She?" Bertha asked.

"The shoe," I said.

"Oh," she said. "You're taking too much for granted, Donald. I still think it's Lamont Hawley."

"I'm beginning to think it may be a woman in Salt Lake," I said. "Anyway Hawley should know about what's happening now."

Bertha said, "Dammit, I was just getting comfortable! I got that goddam girdle off and now I've got to struggle into it again. I wish to hell you could work cases the way other people do. There's no reason on earth why we couldn't build up a respectable, decent agency with the right kind of clients and—"

"You've got the right kind of a client now," I told her. "That is, you told me he was the right kind when *you* closed with him."

"Well, I'm not nearly as sure now as I was a couple of days ago," Bertha said. "If he's hiring one detective agency and then hiring another—fry me for an oyster. I'll fix that bird!"

"All right," I told her. "He's all yours. Fix him."

I crossed over to Bertha's telephone, dialed information and said, "I want the number of Lorraine Robbins of Colinda, please."

Information said, "Just a moment," and a short time later gave me the number. "It's three-two-four, nine-two-four-three. You can dial it from your phone."

"Thanks," I said. I dialed the number and after a moment heard Lorraine Robbins' voice, calmly efficient, saying, "Yes?"

"Lorraine," I said, "this is Donald Lam."

"Oh, yes, Donald."

I said, "I have to see you tonight on a matter of the greatest importance."

"Oh, now *really*, Donald," she said, "when I handed you that line this afternoon I was kidding."

"What line?" I asked innocently.

"I told you that I might *give* you a lot....Look, Donald, it's late and I'm going to bed and...I don't like men who have to take half the night getting their nerve up to—"

"This is business," I said. "This is something that's tremendously important to you and to your employers."

"Can't it keep until office hours?"

"It can't keep."

"What do you want?"

"I want to talk with you."

"All right," she said, "I'll fall for the gag. But now look, Donald, I'm going to tell you something straight from the shoulder. If this is a gag you're using as a build-up, you're going to be wasting an awful lot of time.

"I don't want to have someone ring me up at this hour of the night and tell me it's an emergency business matter and then use the contact as an excuse to start making passes. You're four hours late for passes; no cocktails, no dinner....If you're intending to make passes, say so right now and—"

"It's business, Lorraine," I told her. "I wouldn't have bothered you otherwise."

"I don't know that *that's* so flattering."

"At this hour, I meant. I'd have called you earlier."

"Well, why didn't you?"

"I was busy."

"You're doing better all the time, Donald," she said. "I was just going to bed. I'll be waiting up. Do you have the address?"

"No."

"It's the Miramar Apartments. Two-twelve."

"I'll be there."

"How long?"

"It'll take me a little over half an hour. I'm calling from the city."

"I'll be waiting."

I hung up and saw Bertha's speculative eyes surveying me. "Who was that?"

"Lorraine Robbins," I said. "She's secretary to Holgate and Maxton, the subdividers."

Bertha shook her head. "You sure as hell cover ground," she said.

"That's what I'm paid for," I told her virtuously.

"With women," Bertha added dryly.

There was no use trying to answer that so I walked out and pulled the apartment door shut behind me.

7

Lorraine Robbins answered my ring almost at once. She was dressed in a neat suit and was all business.

"Hello, Donald. Come in. What gives?"

I said, "This Miramar Apartments. Does everyone in Colinda live here?"

"No, why?"

"I know some other people who live here."

"Who?"

"Oh, it isn't *that* important," I said smiling, "but I just wondered why everyone seemed to have this address."

"It's the town's swankiest working girl's apartment house," she said. "It's new, modern and the service is fine. They really keep it warm in the winter and they have air-conditioning in the summer. Yet the rates aren't up in high C. It's quite a job getting in here. They have a waiting list as long as your arm.

"Now, what's bothering you, Donald? Do you want to sit down?"

I seated myself and she went over and sat in a chair across the room and kept her knees together and her skirt down.

I said, "I have to see Mr. Holgate tonight and I want you to be there."

"*You* want me to be there!" she said indignantly. "If Mr. Holgate wants me to—"

"Take it easy," I told her. "This is a matter of considerable importance."

"To whom? To you or to us?"

"To all of us."

"What's it about?"

I said, "That automobile accident. Do you think there's any possibility Mr. Holgate could have been lying about it?"

She said, "In the first place Mr. Holgate doesn't lie. And in the second place there was nothing for him to lie about. He admits liability and his story of the accident coincides with yours."

"Well," I said, "I have reason to believe there's a detective agency working on the thing."

She laughed and said, "Of course there is, silly. There's an insurance company involved and they're trying to find out the nature and the extent of the injuries of this girl that was hit. Oh, *that's* the one you were thinking about! Her address is here in the Miramar Apartments, too. That is, it was. I don't think she's here any more."

"Well," I told her. "I think there's something very much out of the ordinary going on and I'm somewhat alarmed."

"Just what gives you that idea and why are you coming to me with it?"

I reached in my pocket, took out an extra clipping I had cut from the newspaper and said, "I suppose you folks are responsible for this."

"For what?"

"Offering to pay two hundred and fifty dollars for persons who had seen the accident."

She came across the room to take the clipping out of my hand almost before I had a chance to start over toward her. She grabbed the clipping, looked at it, then looked at me.

"*We* didn't put that ad in, Donald. We don't know anything about it."

I said, "My car's down here. Let's go talk to Holgate."

"I'll have to try and locate him," she said. "I've got a couple of night numbers."

I said, "He's out at the subdivision."

"How do you know?"

"I drove past on my way in. The place was all lit up. I thought for a minute of going in and telling him to wait there, that we were coming out as soon as I could pick you up. Then I felt that it wouldn't be but ten or fifteen minutes longer to pick you up and—"

"Well, he may have left the place. You should have stopped in and told him to stay there. Wait a minute and I'll call and—"

"No," I told her, looking at my watch. "There isn't time for that. We're going out there. He's out there. I'm sure he is."

For a moment there was another flicker of suspicion.

"Donald," she said, "you're playing a game. I don't know what it is. If this is an excuse to get me out there and we find the place is all dark and you think you're going to get me in the office and make passes or cuddle up on one of those davenports out there, you just have six more guesses coming.

"When a man makes a pass at me, I want it to be a forward pass. I don't like this lateral pass stuff."

"Okay," I told her, "come on."

She switched out the lights in the apartment, said, "I'm ready."

We went down to my car and I drove in silence. I could see her looking me over carefully. Eventually she shrugged her shoulders and said, "Some difference."

"What's different?" I asked.

"When I was driving you out to the place," she said, "you were looking at me and speculating as to just how far I'd go."

"Well?" I asked.

"Now," she said, "you're doing the driving and I'm looking at you and trying to speculate on how far you've been."

"I've covered a lot of territory," I said.

"Darned if you haven't, and believe me your story had better be good or you're going to find yourself in some mighty hot water.

"If you think you're going to shake Holgate down for two hundred and fifty bucks, you're due to have a surprise. He knows nothing about that ad and he wouldn't pay you a dime."

"I don't want a dime," I said.

She shook her head. "I wish I knew just what you *do* want. You're playing games....I was prepared to like you when I met you and dammit, I still like you."

"Thank you."

"Don't thank me," she said. "It's just the chemistry of the situation. Frankly, I either like them or I don't. I've always been like that. I tell when I get my first exposure to masculine magnetism whether I like or whether I don't like. With you, I liked and I still like, but I'm going to be awfully damned certain where you're expecting to plant your feet before I tell you to jump."

"Fair enough," I told her.

Again we were silent.

I turned off the main road and she could see the lights in the buildings at the subdivision.

"Well," she said, settling back in the seat, "that's a surprise."

"You didn't expect it?"

"No. Frankly, I didn't. I thought you were going to get me out here and suggest we go inside and try and locate Mr. Holgate on the office phone."

"I told you the place was lit up. I could see it from the road."

"Hey, wait a minute," she said. "There aren't any cars here."

"Well, the lights are on. Someone's here."

"I don't get it," she said. "Whoever is here would have a car if he was still here."

"Well, he wouldn't leave without turning off the lights, would he?"

"No."

"Well, then, he's here."

I swung the car around and parked it in front of the door, trying to put it in almost exactly the same spot where I had left it earlier in the evening.

Lorraine jumped to the ground and hurried to the door of the reception room.

She opened the office, walked inside, gave a quick glance at things, then suddenly came to a stop. "Who's been using my typewriter?" she asked.

"What's wrong?" I asked.

"That electric typewriter," she said. "The cover's off and the motor's running."

She went over and put her hand on the machine. I promptly put my hand on the machine and said, "It's been running for some time. It's warm. Perhaps you didn't shut the motor off this afternoon when you quit work."

"Don't be silly," she said. "Somebody's been in here and has been using that typewriter."

She turned and strode toward Holgate's office, put her hand on the knob of the door, stopped, knocked in a perfunctory manner and then opened the door and walked in.

I was right on her heels.

"For God's sake!" she said.

We stood there surveying the wreckage. I said, "Here's a broken compact and—what is this, a powder cake?"

I picked up a piece of the cake.

"That's right. It fell out of the compact."

She took the piece I handed her, sniffed it, looked at it thoughtfully, said, "Probably a blonde."

I moved over to the shoe. "Here's a woman's shoe. Now, what would this mean?"

I picked it up and handed it to her.

"Probably some girl was trying to find a weapon," she said. "She took off the shoe and used the heel."

"Rape?" I asked.

"Not with Holgate."

"How about his partner, Chris Maxton?"

"What do you know about Maxton?"

"What do you?"

"I don't know about his sex habits, if that's what you're leading up to."

I said, "Well, there's evidently been quite a fight here. Someone must have come in through the window."

"Why through the window?"

"It's open."

"Why not *out* through the window?"

"Well," I said, "that's a thought. Let's see."

I sat on the windowsill, then turned and dropped down to the ground, waited there a few moments while she was over inspecting the files that were strewn on the floor. Then I crawled back in the window and said, "A person could get out through the window all right, but why would they do that?"

"Don't ask me," Lorraine said. "I want to know what's happened here and I want to know what's happened to Mr. Holgate."

"And the woman," I said.

"Well, if she lost the fight," Lorraine said, "you can pretty much figure what happened to her. In any event, she's gone."

"Any papers missing?" I asked.

"That's what I'm trying to find out," she said. "There's one paper I'm looking for in particular."

"What's that?" I asked, walking to the lavatory.

She didn't say anything for a while but kept looking through the jackets until she found a manila filing envelope, one of the kind that had a flap and a cord that tied it shut.

She opened the flap, looked inside, then handed the jacket to me. "You take a look," she said.

"But there's nothing in here," I told her.

"Look on the outside of the jacket."

I looked and found in neat feminine handwriting the designation, "Affidavit of Donald Lam, witness to Mr. Holgate's accident."

"*That's* what's missing," she said.

Lorraine reached for the telephone.

"Hold it," I said.

"Hold what?"

"What are you going to do?"

"Notify the sheriff's office."

"Why?"

"Why!" she exclaimed. "Good God, look at this wreckage!"

"All right," I said. "What's been taken?"

"I told you. Your affidavit."

"I'll make you another one."

"What are you getting at?"

I said, "Nothing of value has been taken, at least as far as you know. The place is a wreck, a chair has been smashed, there are a lot of files to clean up.

"You notify the sheriff's office and immediately they come out here and start taking fingerprints. Then the newspapers are notified and there's a lot of publicity. You're working for the firm of Holgate and Maxton. Do you think they'd want that publicity?"

"I don't know."

"Well, let's find out before we blow any whistles."

She thought that over and said, "Donald, you *may* be giving me some pretty darned good advice. Any more suggestions?"

I said, "Let's try to figure out who would want that affidavit bad enough to get in here and smash things up, and who do you suppose had the fight?"

"I wouldn't know."

I said, "It is Holgate's office. There was a fight."

She said, "That's obvious."

I said, "A fight means two people have alternate objectives and they resort to violence to protect their positions."

"Go on," she said.

"It's fairly obvious that one of the persons engaged in the fight must have been Holgate. This is his office. He was either in here when the intruders came in, or the intruders came in and then he came in. Holgate hasn't seen fit to notify the authorities. Therefore, there's no reason why we should."

"You've been over that. I'm sold on that idea."

I said, "I'm trying to find out what the fight was about and what there is about my affidavit that was important enough for somebody to break in and try to locate it."

She said, "Donald, I'm going to tell you something I've never told anybody else. But I want to ask you a question and I want a frank answer."

"Go ahead," I said. "Tell me and then ask the question."

"No," she said, "I'm going to ask the question and *then* I'm going to tell you."

"All right," I told her, "have it your way."

"Donald, are you absolutely certain about that automobile accident?"

"Why, yes," I said. "The thirteenth of August."

"What time?"

"About three-thirty in the afternoon, give or take a few minutes."

"Are you *certain* about the time?"

I watched her face. "I—well, I *could* be a little mistaken. But you know how it is when you're making an affidavit. You don't dare say that it was *about* this or that or the other, or that you *might* be mistaken. If you do that, some attorney will take you on cross-examination and tear the daylights out of you."

She nodded.

"So," I said, "what's wrong with the time?"

She said, "There's a mistake somewhere."

"How do you know?"

She said, "I happen to remember the thirteenth of August because it's my birthday. We had a small office party and a few cocktails that afternoon.

"Now it's true that Mr. Holgate was out during most of the afternoon but he came in shortly after four and joined us for a few minutes, long enough to have a couple of drinks, and then hurried away. He must have had an appointment of some sort. He kept looking at his watch.

"Now the point is that I saw his car at about four-thirty when he drove away and his car wasn't smashed at all."

"You mean the accident is a fake?" I asked. "That the car wasn't smashed and—"

"No, no," she said. "It's the time element, that's all. And I'm not too certain that— Donald, you saw the accident and I want to know whether *you* could have been mistaken."

"I could have been mistaken," I told her.

"Thanks. That's all I want to know."

I said, "We'd better close this window and turn out the lights, hadn't we?"

"And lock up."

I nodded.

"I guess so," she said. She walked around the office, looking things over. "What a holy mess!"

"No use trying to straighten it up tonight," I said. "And in case Mr. Holgate *should* want to have the authorities notified, we should leave things very much the way they are."

"That's right."

I said, "What about the other office? It's dark."

"That's Mr. Maxton's private office."

"Better take a look in there, hadn't we?"

"I suppose so."

"You have a key to it?"

"There's a key in the safe in the outer office."

"And you have the combination to the safe?"

"Of course."

"Let's take a look, just to be on the safe side. The safe doesn't seem to have been tampered with."

We went out to the other office and then she stood regarding her typewriter with frowning concentration. "I just can't understand what happened," she said. "I can't understand who could have been using that typewriter."

"Does Mr. Holgate type?" I asked.

"He can hunt and peck."

"Then somebody must have been here who *could* do some typing or Holgate was trying to type a document."

"I can't imagine who else could have been typing."

"The woman's shoe," I reminded her.

She nodded.

I said, "That gives us a little more to work on. Holgate was here with the woman. He was perhaps selling her a lot She was a typist. In any event, a sale was made and she wanted something written up. Holgate asked her if she could use the typewriter and she said she could so he said to use yours."

Lorraine pursed her lips. "That adds up, Donald. Stay with it. You're doing fine."

"And," I said, "he pointed out your typewriter to her, she took the cover off, turned on the current, put the paper in the machine and started typing."

"Then what?"

"Then," I said, "she had finished with the typing and she brought the paper into Holgate's office for his signature and then was when the intruder came in and started an argument with Holgate. The argument got to the point of a struggle and the girl took off her shoe and tried to rap this man over the head."

Lorraine frowned and shook her head.

"What's wrong with that?" I asked.

"Who won the fight?" she asked.

"Quite obviously the other person," I said.

"All right then, what became of Mr. Holgate and the girl, whoever she was?"

"That," I said, "is something we've got to find out. The man got the paper he wanted. That left Holgate with the girl. He decided that before he notified the authorities, in fact before he did anything, he wanted to go someplace and do something and the girl went with him."

"All right," she said, "carry it a step farther. In that case, the fight must have been over that affidavit of yours."

"Apparently it had something to do with the affidavit, but I don't think whoever went through those papers was looking for the affidavit"

"Well, it's one of the things that's missing."

I said, "Let's try this one for size....The girl came in. Holgate wanted something done in connection with that affidavit.

Perhaps he wanted it copied, perhaps he wanted something in connection with it. He went to the filing case, got the affidavit out of the envelope, and the girl went out to the outer office to start copying and—"

Lorraine snapped her fingers.

"Something clicks?" I said.

"It clicks in a big way," she said. "*That's* what happened. They were working on that affidavit of yours."

"Then the affidavit wasn't the important thing," I said. "The affidavit left the office. It could have left with Holgate and the girl. What the intruder was looking for was something else."

She said, "If the intruder had a chance to do that much searching, he must have had an opportunity when he was more or less undisturbed. That would mean he'd won the fight."

"Sure, he won the fight," I said. "He had to, if we're building it up that way."

"Come on," she said. "Let's go take a look in Maxton's office and then if everything's all right there we'll close this place up and go find Mr. Holgate. Can you stay with me for a while, Donald?"

"For a while," I said.

She said, "What did you want to see him about?"

I said, "Frankly, I was worried about the time element. I wasn't certain when you come right down to it, not absolutely certain, it was three-thirty. I got to thinking it might have been later. I wanted to ask him about it so I could be dead certain."

She said, "The time is wrong. But I know the accident happened because I saw his car."

"When?"

"When it was in the garage being fixed. It was laid up for— oh, I guess a week. They had to get a new radiator and some parts for the front of it."

"When did he tell you about the accident, on the four-teenth?"

She said, "He mentioned it rather casually and—well, he didn't seem to pay too much attention to it. He wrote the insurance company and reported it, and I suggested to him that he'd better notify the police. That was the afternoon of the four-teenth."

I said, "I'd hate to get off on the wrong foot. I fixed the time at three-thirty because that's when Dudley Bedford told me the accident took place according to the police records."

"Just who is Dudley Bedford, Donald?" she asked.

"All I know is that he's the boyfriend of a girl I've met."

"How well do you know *her*?"

"I've just seen her a couple of times."

"Do you expect to see more of her?"

"Probably."

"How much more?"

"That," I said, "depends."

"Is it a girl named Doris Ashley?"

"Yes."

"And Bedford's her boyfriend?"

"I think so. Why do you ask?"

"Because," she said, "Bedford has been in touch with Mr. Holgate, and Mr. Holgate didn't tell me what the conversation was about. Usually he does. It's part of the way he runs the office. He'll tell me all about the various people who come in, give me his impressions of them, let me know what their busi-ness is and all that, so I'll know how to handle myself if they should call up when he isn't in; whether to break my neck trying to locate him or whether to just brush them off.

"But with Bedford, Mr. Holgate just didn't tell me a thing, and of course I didn't ask."

"Well," I said, "I think we'd better look in Maxton's office, then go find Holgate. Let's close up the place here, turn off the lights and see what we can do."

She opened the safe, took out a key. We opened the door to Maxton's office and switched on the light.

The place was neat and orderly.

"Not a thing touched here," she said.

She stood for a moment in thoughtful contemplation, then switched off the light and closed the door.

The spring lock clicked.

She went to the safe, replaced the key, closed the safe door, spun the combination, walked over to her typewriter, switched off the motor and put the plastic cover over the machine.

Then she went into Holgate's office, closed and locked the windows and switched off the lights. We went out, got in my car, and she had me drive to Holgate's apartment.

No one answered the door. The place was dark.

We tried a couple of clubs where he frequently played cards and drew a blank.

"The guy has to be *some*place," I said.

She said, "All right, Donald. He's someplace but we don't know where that someplace is. It's late and I'm going to bed. We'll sleep on it and see what we can find out in the morning."

I looked at her, and her face was just too innocent. I knew damned well she wasn't going to bed and going to sleep. I also knew damned well she wanted to get rid of me in order to look in some other place where she thought Holgate might be found. She didn't want anybody to know where that place was. She was a good secretary.

I rode along with the gag, took her back to her apartment, said good night and drove away.

I circled the block, came back and parked and hadn't been

there more than two minutes when a car came out of the parking lot driving fast.

I got close enough so that when the car went through the lighted intersection I could see it was Lorraine driving. She was all alone in the car.

I didn't try to follow.

I went back to the Perkins Hotel.

There was a note for me to call Doris no matter what time I came in.

I put through the call and a moment later heard Doris' voice on the line.

"Hello," she said cautiously, noncommittally.

"How's tricks?" I asked.

"Donald!" she exclaimed, recognizing my voice. "I thought you were supposed to stay there in the hotel and be where we could reach you with messages."

"Well," I said, "I got sidetracked. It's something I'll have to tell you about later. What's the trouble, anything?"

"I was hoping you'd get in touch with me this evening, Donald, before it got too late."

"Too late for what?"

"For respectability."

"Do we *have* to be respectable?"

"*I* do—in this apartment house."

"Why don't you move?"

She laughed and said, "Seriously speaking, Donald, I thought I was going to see more of you."

"You are."

"When?"

"Tonight?"

"It's too late, Donald. They lock the outer door."

"How about tomorrow?"

"That would be fine. When?"

"The earlier the better. I called you tonight. You didn't answer."

"You called me?"

"Yes."

"Just once?"

"Yes."

"When?"

"I'm not certain about the time. It was at what you'd call a respectable hour."

"Oh, Donald! That must have been when I ran down to the corner to get some cigarettes! Oh, I'm sorry! I was...hoping you'd call. A girl shouldn't say that. It sounds— Oh, hell, Donald, do *we* have to stand on convention?"

"No. Can I come out?"

"Not tonight, Donald. I'd get put out."

"All right, we were talking about tomorrow, early."

She hesitated a moment then said, "I have to go to the airport to meet a friend tomorrow. Why don't you drive out to the airport with me?"

"Your friends," I said, "are sometimes a little violent. I still have a sore jaw."

"That," she said. "I'm very angry about that and believe me, he knows it. No, this isn't a man friend, this is a girl friend. Really I shouldn't let you see her. She's a raving beauty, a blonde with a wonderful figure. She's been back east for a while and she's coming in on the early plane and wants me to meet her."

"Do I know her?" I asked.

"I hope not," she said. "I guess you've heard about her, though. She's Vivian Deshler—you know, the girl who was hurt in that automobile accident."

"Oh, yes," I said, feeling my way cautiously. "That's the accident I saw on the thirteenth of August."

"That's right."

I said, "I've been wondering about the time element of that accident, Doris. Your friend may have given me the wrong time. I think the accident may have been an hour and a half later than—"

"Donald, don't let anyone fool you. The accident was three-thirty."

"How do you know?"

"A friend and I saw Vivian's car at four o'clock. You could see the dent in the rear. She drove out here right after the accident."

"You're sure of the time?"

"Of course."

I said, "Okay, Doris. Why don't I pick you up about eight o'clock? We can have breakfast, then drive to the airport."

"Eight o'clock?"

"Yeah. Is that too early?"

"Heavens, yes. She doesn't get in until ten-forty-five. Come to the apartment at eight-thirty, Donald. I'll have some coffee on and we can have coffee here. Then we can go to the airport and see if the plane's on time, have a little breakfast and then meet her when she comes in."

"You have yourself a breakfast date," I told her. "You're sure it's too late for me to see you tonight?"

"Yes, Donald. Some other night perhaps."

"Some other night for sure," I said, and hung up.

I rang Bertha Cool.

"Donald, Bertha," I said. "What's new?"

"Where are you?"

"Perkins Hotel, Colinda."

"I got hold of a night number for Lamont Hawley," she said, "and I gave him a going over. The guy's completely flabbergasted. He had absolutely no idea any other detective agency was on the job. He swears he didn't try to play one against the other, that all of his dealings with us were on the up and up.

"He seemed tremendously concerned and told me I should tell you to watch your step, that there were things in this case he couldn't understand."

"That," I said, "is an understatement."

"He said that he only got us on the job when he felt that there was, as he expressed it, more to it than met the eye."

"What did you tell him?" I asked.

"I told him plenty," Bertha said grimly. "I told him that if he knew there was more to it than met the eye, he wasn't playing fair with us when he got me to fix the fees and that he was going to have to increase the ante."

"What did he say to that?"

"He never batted an eyelash," Bertha said. "He told me he'd add another thousand dollars to our fees because he hadn't been, as he expressed it, entirely frank."

"With no more trouble than that, he added another thousand bucks to the ante?"

"What the hell do you mean, with no more trouble than that?" Bertha said angrily. "You should have heard what I told the sonofabitch. I went to town."

"Did he ask you how you knew another detective agency was on the job?"

"I told him we'd seen the reports," Bertha said.

"And naturally he wanted to know how you had seen them?"

"Sure."

"What did you tell him?"

"I told him that was none of his business, that we didn't have to explain our methods to anyone; that we were hired to get results, that we'd pass on information but how we got that information was our own affair."

"Well," I told her, "I'm supposed to be here in Colinda tonight but confidentially I'm going home and spend the night in my apartment. I want to get a good night's sleep."

"You don't think you'd get it there?"

"I feel there might be interruptions," I said, "and I want to gain a little time before I have to cope with those interruptions. Also I have an idea I can use a little sleep because it may be the last sleep I'll get for a while."

"All right," Bertha said, "I'm going to bed myself. I was waiting for your call. You've been long enough. What the hell have you been doing?"

"Working on the case."

"I'll bet you had some cutie helping you," Bertha said.

"Why, Bertha!" I exclaimed. "How you talk!" and hung up before she could get in another dig.

I left the hotel, drove the car back to my apartment where I had a private garage, put the car in the garage, closed the door, went up and went to bed.

It was one thing to tell Bertha I was going to have a good night's rest. It was another thing to try and get it.

It was after three o'clock in the morning before I finally got to sleep. The damned case simply didn't make sense, no matter how I looked at it. Holgate and some woman had been having a conference when somebody broke in. There must have been two of those somebodies. Holgate was a big, powerful man. He and a woman between them could have subdued any single individual—unless, of course, that man had a gun, and if he had had a gun there wouldn't have been the evidence of a fight all over the place. Someone would have got shot.

I tossed around in bed, first on one side, then on the other, trying to get to sleep.

I woke up at six feeling just a little more tired than when I had gone to bed and a hell of a lot more frustrated.

8

I showered, shaved, had three cups of strong, black coffee, got in the agency heap and drove to the Perkins Hotel.

There was a message in the box to call Lorraine Robbins at the Miramar Apartments.

I hesitated a moment whether to call her that early but finally decided that as a working girl, she'd be up.

I put through the call and she answered almost instantly. "Donald?"

"That's right."

"Look, Donald, I'm worried about Mr. Holgate."

"It's too early to do any worrying yet, Lorraine. Does he have some appointments this morning?"

"Yes, he has some appointments with important customers."

"Well," I said, "wait until you see if he keeps those appointments. For all we know, he may be in his apartment sleeping off a convivial evening."

"He isn't," she said. "He isn't anywhere."

"What do you mean, anywhere, and how do you know he isn't in his apartment? Perhaps he isn't answering the phone."

"I've been up to his apartment, Donald. The bed hasn't been slept in."

"How did you get in?"

"The manager knows me. I told him that I had some important papers that I had to deliver and asked if he'd open up the apartment for me."

"What would you have done if you'd found Holgate snuggled in bed with some beautiful babe?"

"I don't know," she said, "but I had a definite feeling he wasn't snuggled in any bed with any beautiful babe. I knew what I'd find."

"What did you find?"

"The bed hadn't been slept in. No one was there—and of course I wasn't foolish enough to go into the bedroom while the manager was there. Mr. Holgate has a very fine three-room apartment."

"Everything seemed to be in order? Any indication the place had been ransacked?"

"No. Everything was in order."

"All right," I said, "when I left you last night, did you go right to bed?"

"Why?"

"I want to know."

"Why?"

"Because I want to know what advice to give you. You are asking me whether you should notify the police. It could be very embarrassing to your boss if the police should be notified and it turned out he was simply on a social engagement."

"All right, Donald, I'll be frank with you. There was one place where I thought he might be, one apartment."

"And you got the young lady up out of—"

"Don't be silly, I was looking for his car. If he'd been there, his car would have been parked near the apartment house. I went out and covered the place thoroughly. His car wasn't there."

"Then what?"

"I called his apartment two or three times during the night and of course got no answer. I'm worried."

I said, "Wait until those appointments come up. If he doesn't keep the appointments, and they're important ones, you'll know that the police had better be notified."

"Well," she said somewhat reluctantly, "the first appointment is at ten o'clock. I don't like to wait until then but…well, I guess it *is* the best thing to do.

"Are you going to be around here today, Donald?"

"I'll be in and out. I'll keep in touch with you. You'll be at the office?"

"After nine o'clock, yes."

"I'll either drop in and see you or give you a buzz," I said.

I hung up, waited until eight-twenty and drove out to the Miramar Apartments. I had no trouble finding a parking place and tapped on the door of Doris Ashley's apartment promptly at eight-thirty.

She had on a filmy negligee and as she opened the door the light from the apartment silhouetted her figure through the diaphanous, fluffy folds of the garment.

"Donald!" she said. "You're early!"

"Eight-thirty?" I said.

"That's what I told you, eight-thirty, but it's only eight o'clock and—"

"Eight-thirty," I said.

"What!" she exclaimed. "My alarm clock just went off. I set it for quarter to eight."

I looked at the alarm clock by the bed. It now registered two minutes past eight o'clock.

I said, "What did you set it by last night?"

"The alarm? I set it at seven-forty-five."

"No, when you wound the clock and set it, what did you set it by?"

"Why, by the television. I was watching a program and—"

"You set it half an hour slow."

"I couldn't have! Let me see your watch."

She came over and stood close to me, and I held my wrist watch up so she could see it.

She took my wrist in her hands, held my arm close to the negligee, said, "Well, for heaven sakes, what do you know!" She stood there for a moment, then said, "Donald, I've got to get some clothes on. There's coffee in the percolator in the kitchenette. Will you keep an eye on it and I'll...I'll get some clothes on right quick. I'll run in the closet and dress."

She made a dash for the closet, stripping off the negligee as she opened the door.

I had occasional tantalizing glimpses of her moving past the door, attired in panties and bra, and then she was out in the apartment with street clothes and neatly shod feet.

I gave a little wolf whistle.

"Donald!" she said. "Get your mind on what we have to do."

I said, "It's a little difficult....Those are certainly neat shoes. What are they, alligator skin?"

"Yes. I like alligator skin. I'm very partial to it. I like alligator skin and a brown shade of stockings."

She raised her skirt a little, looked up at me and smiled. "You like?"

"I like."

She said, "I'm ravenously hungry. I was only going to have a cup of coffee but I think I've got to have some toast and just a little bacon. Do you suppose there's time?"

"Oh, sure there's time," I said. "We'll make it down okay; in fact we could have breakfast here if you wanted."

"No, I like to eat at the airport while we're waiting but we could have just a snack here."

She hurried out to the kitchen.

I walked over to the closet where she had been dressing.

Feminine garments were hanging in the closet and there was an open drawer filled with intimate feminine lingerie.

I found a rack of shoes at the end of the closet and hastily picked up one of the alligator shoes and looked at the place of manufacture.

It was Chicago, Illinois.

I picked up another one. That was Salt Lake City, the same shoe store that had been stamped in the shoe I had found at Holgate's office.

"Donald, where are you?" she asked.

I hurried out of the closet.

"Coming," I told her.

"Do you want to make the toast while I cook the bacon? I have an electric bacon cooker here that is supposed to get it just right—and there's an electric toaster. There's some bread in there."

I got the bread out of the breadbox, dropped two slices in the electric toaster and pushed down the lever which made the contact.

The electric bacon broiler did its stuff, and the aroma of bacon and coffee mingled in the little breakfast nook.

"Donald," she said, "I'm sorry about Dudley."

"That's all right."

"He…he took advantage of you. I wouldn't have had that happen—well, I know that he put you in a position where you had to say you had seen that accident."

"I've got news for you, Doris," I told her.

"What?"

"I *did* see the accident."

The platter she was holding over the stove to warm all but slipped from her hands. "You *what!*" she exclaimed.

"I saw that damned accident," I said. "It was just one of

those peculiar, crazy coincidences that wouldn't happen in a million years. Of course I didn't have the faintest idea at the time that you were interested in it or were ever going to be interested in it, but—well, it happened. I saw it, that's all."

She hesitated a moment, recovered her self-possession, put the bacon on the platter and laughed throatily.

"Donald," she said, "you *are* a card. It's all right, Donald, you don't have to fool me. You know, Vivian is the girl who was involved in that accident and—well, she's probably going to ask you about it."

"Is that why you wanted me to meet her?"

"Heavens, no. I wanted to see you, that's all. I— Donald, why didn't you call me more than once last night?"

"I did, but you weren't home."

"I told you I was getting cigarettes."

"I called you again, and again. You didn't answer."

"Why, Donald, you must have had the wrong number. I was sitting right here by that telephone the whole blessed evening —and I made an excuse to get rid of Dudley."

"He wasn't here?"

"No."

"You weren't together?"

"No, and I'll tell you something else, Donald. I don't know that I'm going to be with him too much. I became involved with him and—well, it's getting to a point where it's leading to things I don't like. Dudley is—well, he's possessive and he's ruthless. You've probably seen enough of him to realize that."

I looked at her shoes. "You certainly have pretty feet."

She laughed and made a playful kick. "Can't you get your mind on anything higher than my feet?"

"You buy these shoes here?"

"No. These were given to me by a girlfriend. Why do you ask?"

"Your girlfriend from Salt Lake?"

She showed surprise. "She lived there for a while. Why, Donald?"

"I like shoes."

"You're not one of those goofs that go crazy over women's clothes, are you, Donald—women's panties and things like that? I've heard that when men are shut up in prison their sex drive sometimes takes strange slants. Donald, tell me about it."

"About what?"

"What it's like to live without women."

"It's hell."

"Do you go crazy when you get out? Sex crazy, I mean?"

"Yes."

"You don't act like it."

"I've forgotten how to act."

"I'll have to give you a memory course. In the meantime we have a plane to meet.

"Now, take your bacon and put it right on the toast, Donald, and then put another piece of toast on top and make a toasted bacon sandwich. It's a wonderful breakfast—only we'll have another breakfast out at the airport. This will be a breakfast hors d'oeuvre, kind of a preliminary. Do you like preliminaries, Donald?"

"I love them."

"Sometimes," she said somewhat wistfully, "I think the pre-liminaries are more interesting than the…" She hesitated, trying to find the word she wanted.

"The main event?" I asked.

She laughed and said, "You certainly have a quick wit. Do you like cream and sugar in your coffee?"

"Not now," I said. "Later on when we have breakfast at the airport. Now I'm drinking it black."

"You look wonderful this morning, Donald. Did you sleep last night?"

"Like a top," I said. "How about you?"

"I had a wonderful night's rest."

"You look fresh as a daisy."

"Do I really?"

"You sure do."

"Donald, I'm glad we got acquainted. I would like to do things for you—well, I feel that you have had the breaks go against you and you've been sort of—well, you're shy…"

"What do you mean, shy?"

"A little while ago, when I was holding your arm, looking at your wristwatch—well, considering the circumstances most men would have crushed me to them."

I said, "I don't work that way."

"You mean you don't crush women to you impulsively?"

"No," I said, "I don't like to try to make passes at a woman with one eye on an alarm clock and my mind on the schedule of an incoming airplane. I like soft lights, dreamy music, an atmosphere of leisure and privacy and—"

"Donald, stop it!"

I looked at my wristwatch. "All right," I told her. "Do we wash the dishes before we go to the airport?"

"We certainly do," she said. "I hate to come home to a sinkful of dirty dishes. I always like to keep the apartment neat as a pin. But I just use hot water and just a slight touch of detergent. Thank heavens they have really hot water in this apartment. It's steaming."

She turned hot water into the sink, put in a few drops of detergent, took a dish mop, washed the dishes, rinsed them and handed them to me.

"You wipe," she said.

I wiped.

We were ready to leave at twelve minutes past nine.

Doris gave a quick look around the apartment, said, "You're going to like Vivian, but don't you go falling for her, Donald. I'm not ready to share you—not just yet."

"Vivian's good-looking?" I asked.

"A knockout. Blonde and lots of this and that and these and those."

"You're going to ride with me?" I asked.

"Uh-huh."

"All right, my car's down in front. Let's go."

She looked at the alarm clock and laughed. "Can you imagine me being so stupid?" she said.

She went over and moved the hands thirty minutes ahead.

"How's that, Donald, right?"

"Right."

"All right, let's go."

I held the door of the apartment open for her and she walked out past me, elevating her chin and giving me a provocative smile as she brushed past me in the doorway.

We went down in the elevator, got in the agency car, drove to the airport and checked on the plane Vivian was coming in on. It was marked on time.

We went up to the restaurant and had sausage, scrambled eggs and more coffee.

I found the gate that Vivian's plane was coming in, and Doris and I walked out to meet her.

The plane arrived on time and taxied up to a stop.

Passengers started streaming out, and I spotted Vivian before Doris needed to say a word.

She was a striking blonde in a short raw silk sheath suit of shocking-pink. The unbuttoned jacket swung open to reveal a low-cut neck. The dress itself would have been sacklike on a less well-developed model. Her figure gave it what it needed.

"There's Vivian now," Doris said, jumping up and down with synthetic eagerness.

Vivian came through the gate, and Doris gave a little squeal of delight and ran and grabbed her in her arms.

"Vivian!" she said. "You're looking wonderful!"

Vivian smiled, a slow, languid smile. "Hello, sexpot," she said.

"Don't call me that, Vivian, I've—I have someone here."

She turned to me. "Donald, this is Vivian. Vivian, may I present Donald Lam, a friend of mine."

"The latest?" Vivian asked.

"Absolutely the latest."

Vivian looked me over, then slowly extended her hand. "Hello, Donald," she said in a deep, velvety voice.

There was a slow, deliberate motion in the way she extended her hand that made the gesture seem significant. It was the way a trained strip-teaser can take off gloves so that the action seems packed with dynamite and a bare arm from the elbow to the fingertips seems an immoral display of naked flesh.

"Donald drove me out," Doris explained. "Heavens, Vivian, you must have left there at all hours."

"There's a three-hour time difference," she said. "And I had to take a puddle-jumper with stops in Chicago, Denver and Salt Lake. It's two o'clock in New York right now. I don't mind telling you, darling, I left in the small hours of the morning."

"How in the world did you ever get up?"

"That's easy," Vivian said smiling. "I didn't go to bed."

She opened her purse, took out her airplane ticket, detached the baggage stubs, started to hand them to me, then said, "Donald, why don't you go get the car, and I'll have a porter rustle up the baggage. You can drive up, in front of the loading zone and they won't bother you just so you raise the lid of the trunk and leave it up. You can park there twenty minutes if you have to, just keep the trunk open and stand by it expectantly." Her deep blue eyes rested on mine. "Can you look expectant, Donald?"

"I don't know," I said. "When I've been expectant I've never looked at myself."

"He says the cutest things," Doris said.

Vivian let her eyes play with mine. "Look expectant for me now, Donald."

"I might be disappointed."

"You *might* be."

"Donald, you go get the car," Doris said.

Vivian said, "Don't be in too big a hurry, Donald. It'll take ten or fifteen minutes for them to get the baggage off and it'll take me a minute or two to get it picked out and have a porter get it out to the car."

"I'll tell her all about you while you're gone, Donald," Doris Ashley said. "That is, not *all*, but almost all. And I'll also tell her, no poaching on my preserves."

She smiled amiably at Vivian. "You may trespass, honey, but don't poach."

"Where's the fence?" Vivian asked.

I went to get the car.

It was a long walk to where I had parked it and it took me a few minutes to get through the parking lot, then drive around to a place in front of the baggage unloading zone.

They'd evidently been more expeditious than Vivian had anticipated. They were waiting there with a porter, four suitcases and a handbag.

The baggage was neatly stacked on one of the hand trucks and I handed the trunk key to the porter.

I walked over and held the door open for the girls.

"We can sit in front," Vivian said, and promptly started for the middle position in the front seat.

It was at that moment I heard the yell from the porter.

I turned around.

The porter was standing riveted, his eyes big as teacups. He let out another yell, turned and started running as fast as he could pump his legs up and down.

"Now, what the hell!" Doris said. "What did you do to him, Donald?"

I walked to the rear of the car.

I saw something in the trunk, something dark. It looked like a trousers leg.

I stepped hurriedly to the rear and got a good look.

The body of Carter J. Holgate was doubled up in a knees-to-chest position inside the trunk.

It needed only one look at him to know that he was dead.

I heard Doris Ashley's scream in my ears and then the sound of a police whistle. After that people were crowding all around, women were screaming and a police officer was holding me by the arm.

"This your, car, Buddy?" he asked.

"This is my car," I said.

The officer said, "Keep back, you folks. I don't want anybody around here."

He blew a whistle.

A man in some sort of uniform connected with the airport came hurrying forward, and a moment later I heard a siren, and a radio car came speeding up, then slowed to a crawl as it pushed its way through the crowd.

Two uniformed officers jumped out, and I found myself bundled into the radio car. Two minutes later I was in an office at the airport with the officers questioning me, and a man in civilian clothes taking notes.

"What's your name?" one of the officers asked.

I told him.

"Let's see your driving license."

I gave it to him.

"This your car?"

"It's the agency car."

"What were you doing out here?"

"Meeting a girl who was coming in on a plane."

"What's her name?"

I told him.

"What was the flight number?"

I gave him that information.

"Who's the man in your trunk?"

I said, "From the look I had, I think he's Carter J. Holgate but I can't be certain."

"Who's Carter Holgate?"

"A real estate agent, a subdivider."

"You know him?"

"Of course I know him. Otherwise I wouldn't know who he was."

"When did you see him last?"

"Sometime yesterday, late yesterday afternoon."

"How did the body get in the trunk of your car?"

"I wish I knew."

"Anything else?"

I said, "A lot else. I have been talking with Lorraine Robbins. She—"

"Who's she?" the officer interrupted.

"Carter Holgate's secretary."

"Where does she live?"

"Miramar Apartments, Colinda."

"All right, what were you talking with her about?"

"About Holgate. She was worried about him."

"She evidently had good reason to be. What did she say?"

"He hadn't been home all night and she was worried."

"She living with him?"

"No. She knew he was missing."

"How did she know he was missing?"

"We tried to locate him last night."

"You say, *we* did?"

"That's right."

"You were with her?"

"Part of the time."

"And what were you trying to do?"

"We were trying to locate Carter Holgate."

"Why?"

"Because someone had broken into his office."

"What time was that?"

"You mean when we were looking for him? I don't know. I didn't notice the time particularly. I know it was late. Probably after midnight."

"How did you know someone had broken into his office?"

"Because we were in his office."

"What were you looking for?"

"Holgate."

"Why?"

"I had some things I wanted to discuss with him."

"What?"

"An automobile accident."

"What about it?"

"I don't know whether I care to make a statement about the accident at this time."

"Look, Buddy," the officer said, "you're in bad. You're a private detective. You're smart enough to know the spot you're in. You'd better come clean."

"I'm coming clean."

"Not if you hold out about an accident, you aren't."

I said, "What happened to the girls who were in the automobile with me?"

"Here at the airport?"

"Yes."

"They're being questioned."

I said, "One of them, the blonde, was involved in the accident."

"What's her name?"

"Vivian Deshler."

"What's the other's name?"

"Doris Ashley."

"When did you get in touch with her?"

"This morning."

"What time?"

"Eight-thirty."

"Where?"

"At her apartment."

"What for?"

"So we could drive out here and meet Miss Deshler."

"What about Holgate's office being broken into?"

"There was pretty much of a wreck there, as though a fight had taken place in the office."

"That was reported to the authorities?"

"I don't think so."

"Why not?"

"His secretary thought that it might be better to wait."

"Wait for what?"

"Wait to see what happened this morning."

"Well, it happened this morning all right," the officer said. "Now, we've got some work to do and some things to check. I want you to sit down here at this desk and write out just what you've told me. Write everything you know about the case."

I said, "Look, do you know Sergeant Frank Sellers?"

"Sure, we know him."

"I know him, too," I said. "Get hold of Sellers and I'll talk with him. In the meantime, I'm not going to do any writing."

"You're not going to do what?"

"Not going to do any writing."

"You know what that means, Buddy. You're leading with your chin."

"All right, I'll lead with my chin. But I'll talk with Sellers and in the meantime I'm not doing any writing."

"Okay, we'll call Sellers. We'll probably take you up there."

An officer went to the telephone and talked in a low voice for a while. I couldn't hear what he was saying. Then I was left alone in the room for what must have been twenty minutes.

Then two officers came in, bringing Doris Ashley and Vivian Deshler.

The officer got right down to business.

"You girls sit down over here," he said.

Doris gave me a reassuring smile.

Vivian Deshler looked me over speculatively.

"Now then, Lam," the officer said, "you saw an automobile accident in Colinda on the thirteenth of August."

"What of it?"

"Describe the accident."

"Well, it was just an accident where somebody ran into the rear of the automobile in front."

"Who was that somebody?"

"Carter Holgate."

"Who was in the car in front?"

"Miss Deshler, here."

"You're positive?"

"Of course, I didn't know her at the time but now that I've seen her I know she's the one."

"All right, describe the accident."

"Well, that's about all there was to it."

"Go ahead, describe it. How did it happen?"

"Well," I said, "there was a string of cars."

"How big a string?"

"I think there were two ahead of Miss Deshler's car and then, of course, Holgate's car was right behind hers."

"So that would make four all together?"

"Right."

"All right, what happened?"

"Well, they approached the intersection."

"What intersection?"

"Seventh and Main in Colinda."

"Where were you?"

"I was on the west side of Main Street."

"How far back from the intersection?"

"Probably seventy-five or a hundred feet."

"What happened?"

"I think Holgate had been trying to speed up to get around the line of automobiles ahead. When he saw he couldn't make it, he tried to get back in line and he was going pretty fast."

"Why couldn't he make it?"

"Well, I guess he wanted to get in the left-hand lane so he could pass while the signal was in his favor and—"

"And he saw he couldn't make it?"

"I guess so. I couldn't read his mind. All I could tell was what happened from the way he drove the car."

"The reason he couldn't make it, then, must have been that the traffic signal was changing."

"Could be."

"Then he was watching the signal."

"I wouldn't know."

"The only other reason would have been that there were cars in front of him on the left."

"I don't remember any cars in front of him on the left."

"And what happened when the signal changed?"

"The car that was approaching the intersection could have gone through on the yellow light but the driver stopped suddenly. So the car behind him stopped very suddenly, almost collided with him. Miss Deshler was driving a lighter car. She brought it to a stop, and Holgate evidently didn't see she had stopped until right at the last minute. He slammed on his brakes hard just about three feet before he hit, but that didn't do anything except slow down his car somewhat. He hit the Deshler car a pretty good lick and I could see Miss Deshler's head snap back."

The officer looked at her.

Vivian Deshler sized me up slowly and thoughtfully and then said, "He's a liar."

"Why is he a liar?" the officer asked.

"That wasn't the way the accident happened at all."

"How did it happen?" I asked.

"There were two lanes of automobiles approaching the intersection," she said. "I was in the left lane. Mr. Holgate had been in the right lane. There were four or five cars in the right lane and only one car ahead of me in the left lane. Mr. Holgate tried to get in the left lane so he could go around the string of cars in the right lane. He was going pretty fast. He swung out to the left, right in behind me, and the signal changed and he hit me."

"How many cars ahead of you when you came to the intersection?" the officer asked.

"None," she said. "I was the only car on the left. There were five or six cars on the right. That's why Mr. Holgate tried to get around the string of cars on the right and make a run for it. He must have been speeding up until just before he hit me. I could see him coming in the rearview mirror."

"All right, Lam," the officer said. "You didn't see the accident. Now why did you say you did?"

Doris Ashley spoke up. "I'll tell you why," she said. "Because Dudley Bedford forced him to make a statement."

"What do you mean, he forced him?"

Doris said, "I could get killed for telling you this."

"Nobody's going to kill you for telling *us* anything," the officer said. "What happened?"

She said, "Donald Lam is a dear. He was in San Quentin. He got out and was trying to get a job where he could go straight and Dudley Bedford, for reasons of his own, forced Donald Lam to make an affidavit that he had seen this accident."

The officer looked at her thoughtfully. "Now," he said, "*I'll* tell *you* something. Donald Lam is a private detective. He's a member of the partnership of Cool and Lam. He's taking you all for a ride. He's never been in San Quentin—yet. He was trying to play on your sympathies. Miss Ashley, and I don't know what he was trying to do with you, Miss Deshler, but…"

The door opened and Frank Sellers walked into the room. "Hello, Frank," I said.

"Hello, Pint Size," Sellers said. "What the hell have you been doing this time?"

"Trying to make a living," I said.

"You should leave murder out of it," he said.

He turned to the officer. "What's going on here?"

The officer said, "We just caught him in a lie, Sergeant."

"That's nothing," Sellers said. "You can catch him in a dozen of them and then the little bastard will squirm right out of them. And, if you're not careful, leave you holding the sack."

"Any time I left you holding the sack," I told Sellers, "there was something in it that you wanted."

"We won't go into that," Sellers said. He nodded to the officer. "Come on, let's get these girls out of here. We'll talk for a minute and you can give me the lowdown. Then I'll come back and question this guy."

They all left the room.

It was a good twenty minutes before Sellers came back alone.

He was chewing the soggy butt of a cold cigar and he looked at me thoughtfully.

"You *do* do the damnedest things, Lam," he said.

"I have the damnedest things done to me," I told him.

"Did you see that automobile accident?"

"No."

"Why did you say you did?"

"Because this man, Bedford, was forcing me to make an affidavit."

"How did he force you?"

"He knocked me over, for one thing."

"And then what?"

"Well, he had the idea I'd been in San Quentin and I rode along with the gag."

"Why?"

"I wanted to see what *his* interest was in the deal."

"All right, there was another fellow, a man by the name of Chris Maxton, Carter Holgate's partner. You made a statement to him about seeing the accident and got paid two hundred and fifty bucks for it."

"That's right."

"And why did you do that?"

"I wanted to see why they were offering two hundred and fifty bucks for witnesses and who was paying the money."

Sellers shook his head and said, "I'm surprised at a smart guy like you taking the two hundred and fifty bucks, Donald. That makes it obtaining money under false pretenses."

"And that makes me guilty of murder?" I asked.

"No," Sellers said, "other things make you guilty of murder."

"Such as what?"

"Such as being in Holgate's office, jumping out the window, running to your car, which already had Holgate's body stuffed in the trunk, and making a getaway."

"Who says so?"

"Your fingerprints say so."

"What are you talking about?"

"Talking about the fingerprints you left in Holgate's place of business," Sellers said. "This Lorraine Robbins tried her best to cover up for you. She said she went out there with you and that was when you first discovered what had happened, but your fingerprints say you were lying to her."

"What do you mean, my fingerprints?"

Sellers grinned and said, "It was a slick stunt, Donald. You went back the second time and pretended to discover what had happened. You were being very, very helpful with Lorraine and you got your fingers all over everything so that the fingerprints you'd left the first time wouldn't be significant. But you overlooked one thing."

"What?"

"The woman's shoe."

"What about it?"

"When that papier-mâché model of the subdivision fell off the table, it hit the shoe. You can see the mark on the leather where the shoe was halfway under it."

"I wouldn't know anything about that," I said.

"And," Sellers said, "you lifted up the papier-mâché model in order to pull the shoe out and look at it."

I shook my head.

"And," Sellers said, "when you did, you left the print of your middle finger outlined in the powder you had got on your finger from the broken compact *on the underside of the papier-mâché model*. An investigation started out there at nine this morning."

Sellers quit talking and shifted the cold cigar butt around in his mouth.

"Now let's see you talk your way out of *that* one, Pint Size."

I didn't say anything.

"Well?" Sellers asked at length.

I said, "You're getting way out on a limb, Sergeant. I could have got my fingerprint on the underside of that papier-mâché at any time."

"No, you couldn't," he said. "After the shoe was taken out and that papier-mâché model got down flat on the floor, there was no place to get your finger under it. You couldn't even pick it up unless you used the blade of a screwdriver or a chisel or something of that sort to slide under it and lift it up. The thing weighs over a hundred pounds. We couldn't lift it and you couldn't."

"I see," I said. "I'm guilty as hell, is that right?"

"We don't know. We're investigating."

I said, "You're a hell of an investigator. You find my finger-print on the underside of a papier-mâché subdivision model weighing a hundred pounds, so you immediately come to the conclusion that I broke into Holgate's office, licked Holgate, clubbed him into unconsciousness, pulled him out of the window, dragged him across the lawn, put him in the trunk of my automobile and then went back for something. What did I go back for, another body?"

"Perhaps you wanted that affidavit you'd signed after you found out it was cockeyed," Sellers said.

"And if I couldn't move one side of a papier-mâché model, just how did I pick up the two-hundred-and-twenty-five-pound Holgate in my arms, jump out of the window with him, carry him across to the car and put him in the trunk?"

"We don't know," Sellers said. "We intend to find out."

"It should be worthwhile finding out," I told him. "If I could carry a two-hundred-and-twenty-five to two-hundred-and-fifty-pound man out of the window and put him in the trunk of my car, it would seem that I should be able to pick up one end of a papier-mâché subdivision model that only weighed a hundred pounds in all."

"You *could* have had an accomplice, you know," Sellers said. "You only needed to carry half of the load."

"That makes it fine," I said. "Who was my accomplice?"

"We're looking around," Sellers said, chewing thoughtfully on the cigar.

"All right, where does that leave me? Am I charged with murder?"

"Not yet."

"Am I under arrest?"

"Not yet."

"What *is* happening?"

"You're being held for questioning."

I shook my head and said, "I don't like that. Either charge me or turn me loose."

"We can hold you for questioning."

"You've questioned me. I want to use the phone."

"Go right ahead," he said.

I walked over to the telephone, called the office and told the office operator to get me Bertha Cool on the line fast.

When I heard Bertha's voice saying, "All right, what is it *this* time?" I said, "I'm being questioned about the murder of Carter Holgate. I'm out at the airport. Holgate's body was found in the trunk of our automobile. I've got work to do. I want to—"

Bertha interrupted me. "Holgate's body!" she screamed.

"That's right," I explained patiently, "his murdered body. It was found jammed into the trunk of the agency car."

"The *agency* car!" she yelled.

"That's right," I said. "Now, Sellers is here. He's questioning me and I've got work to do. I've told him all I know. I want him either to charge me with murder or release me. He doesn't want to do either right at the moment. I want you to get the best lawyer in the city to file *habeas corpus* proceedings."

Bertha said, "You let *me* talk with Frank Sellers."

I held the phone out to Sergeant Sellers. "She wants to talk with you, Frank."

Sellers grinned and said, "Tell her it won't be necessary. I'm protecting my left eardrum. Tell her we're turning you loose."

I said into the telephone, "Sellers said it isn't necessary. He says he's turning me loose."

"What does that mean?"

"It means I'm coming to the office," I said.

Sellers said, "You aren't driving your car anymore, Donald.

That's being impounded for evidence, bloodstains and all of that."

I told Bertha on the telephone, "Sellers is impounding the car. I'll get a cab."

"A cab, my eye! Get one of those damned limousines and save four dollars."

"This is murder," I told her. "Minutes count."

"Minutes be damned!" Bertha said. "Dollars count, too."

"And," I told her, "get our client to come to the office. I want him there."

"And put out a chair for me," Sellers said.

"How's that?" I asked.

"Put out a chair for me. I'm going to be with you. If you're going to get a smart lawyer to file *habeas corpus*, we aren't going to lead with our chins. We aren't going to charge you with murder before we know what kind of a case we have, but I'm going to be with you, Donald, just like a brother."

"You tell Bertha," I said.

"You tell her," he told me.

I said, "Sellers is going to be with me. They aren't ready to charge me with murder but Sellers is going to stick with me, at least that's what he says."

Bertha said, "Can we stop him?"

"Probably not," I said. "That's the way the police act. They'll either insist on having someone with me or they'll put me in custody and charge me with suspicion of murder. They can hold me for a while on that."

Bertha thought that over for a minute, then said, "We'll make that sonofabitch pay half the taxi fare if he's going to ride with you."

"We can probably do better than that," I said. "I think he has a police car. You get our client there in the office. I want to talk with him."

"And I want to listen," Sellers said, grinning. "This is getting better and better."

"How soon will you be here?" Bertha asked.

"Right away," I told her. "You get the interview all set up."

I hung up.

Sellers was still grinning.

"I told them you'd do just that," Sellers said.

"What?"

"Threaten to get *habeas corpus*," Sellers said, "to force our hand, and that we could just give you all the rope you wanted, and you'd lead us to all the people we wanted."

9

We gathered in Bertha's office: Frank Sellers, chewing on a fresh cigar, smugly satisfied with his cleverness; Bertha Cool, gimlet-eyed, cautious, playing them close to her chest; and Lamont Hawley, calm, dignified, reserved, quite evidently wishing to keep out of the whole mess as much as possible.

"All right, Pint Size," Sellers said. "This is your party. You've called it. Start addressing the chair."

He grinned at Bertha Cool.

Bertha Cool's eyes blazed back at him. "The idea of you trying to pin a murder on Donald Lam, Frank Sellers!" she stormed.

"He's trying to pin it on himself," Sellers said, "and the more wading he does, the deeper in he gets. It'll be over his head pretty quick."

"I've heard you talk that way before," Bertha said, "and by the time the smoke blew away Donald was right and you were riding along on his coattails to get a lot of credit you didn't deserve. What's more, that goddam cigar of yours stinks. Throw it away."

Sellers said, "I like the taste of it, Bertha."

"Well, I don't like the smell of it."

"I'll take it out if you want."

"Well, take it out!" Bertha stormed.

Sellers got up and started for the door.

"Hey, wait a minute. Where are you going to throw it? There's no place to throw that cigar out in—"

"Who said anything about throwing it?" Sellers asked innocently. "You said you wanted me to take it out. I was just going to take it out."

"And take yourself with it?"

"Why, sure."

"You sit down in that chair," Bertha Cool said, "and you can listen for a minute and not be so damned smart. Now Donald, what the hell is this all about?"

I turned to Lamont Hawley. "You didn't get the Ace High Detective Agency on the job?"

"No. I told Mrs. Cool all about that."

"Why did you get me on the job?"

"I see no reason for going into that all over again, Lam, particularly in the presence of witnesses and since anything I may say here may be repeated in the press.

"I don't mind telling you—both of you—that my company looks with considerable disfavor on the inevitable publicity which will result from retaining you to investigate this accident.

"As you may be aware, and can readily understand if you give it *any* thought, we don't court publicity in these matters and—"

"That's a lot of double-talk," I interrupted. "Why did you get us in this case instead of using your own investigative setup?"

"I've explained it a dozen times," Hawley said.

"Try making it thirteen," I said. "Sergeant Sellers might be interested."

Hawley sighed patiently. "Sergeant, I don't know how *you* feel about this but it seems to me Mr. Lam is sparring for time."

"Let him spar," Sellers said. "We've got lots of it. And he'll have lots of it. Maybe a life sentence—*if he's lucky*."

I said to Hawley, "We're waiting."

Hawley said, "We felt that an outside agency could give us perhaps better coverage."

I said, "Come again."

"You heard me," Hawley said.

"I heard you," I told him, "and it didn't make any sense. You wanted an outside agency for some reason. Was it because you were afraid of a libel and slander suit?"

His eyes narrowed.

"Was it?" I asked.

Hawley started to say something, then changed his mind. Sellers, who had been watching Hawley with the shrewd eyes of a cop who has seen lots of people under interrogation, said, "You don't like notoriety, Hawley. I think you've had a fair question. Why not answer it here instead of at the D.A.'s office with the newspapermen hanging around the door looking for information and wondering why your insurance company got dragged into the thing?"

Hawley flushed and said, "That is one of the annoying features of this whole case."

I said to Sellers, "My best guess is that the thing got too hot for them to handle. They had to make accusations against Holgate and they didn't want to take the responsibility of doing it. It was worth some money to them to have an independent agency stick its neck out."

Sellers turned to Hawley, took the cigar out of his mouth and pointed the end at him. "Anything to it, Hawley?"

Hawley, who had been doing a lot of thinking, suddenly changed his tactics. "There's nothing to it in the way he expresses it, Sergeant. However, I will say this. Certain things about the way the claim for injuries was handled by Vivian Deshler led us to believe that we might be dealing with a professional setup."

"What do you mean, a professional setup?"

"Well, the symptoms were listed with great detail, and in the offer of settlement which she submitted the itemization of the various amounts of pain and suffering and nervousness, the description of the symptoms and all of that, led us to believe we might be dealing with a malingerer."

"Just because she made a claim?"

"It was the way the claim was made. Our adjuster had been a little bit undiplomatic and had made a statement in the presence of witnesses which bothered us. It could have been the foundation for some sort of action unless he had been able to prove his insinuation, and apparently there wasn't much chance of doing that with the information we had available at the time or felt we could get with reasonable luck."

Sellers turned to me. "That answer your question, Pint Size?"

"It detours it," I said.

"All right," Sellers said. "Let's go on from there. What's your next answer?"

I said, "The next answer is, there wasn't any accident."

"What do you mean, there wasn't any accident?" Lamont Hawley said. "Of course there was an accident. We checked the garage that repaired Holgate's car and we checked the garage that repaired the Deshler car. They even had a part of the Deshler fender that had been removed and the paint that was on it came from Holgate's car. You're going to have to do better than that, Lam."

Sellers grinned and said, "Keep squirming, Lam. I like to watch you. You're like a trout I landed last summer, a great big trout. I got him in the net and he fought like hell. He squirmed and flopped and thrashed his tail around but he wasn't getting anyplace. He was in the net."

Sellers chuckled at the recollection.

I said, "Don't you see it yet? There wasn't any accident. Carter

Holgate got drunk. He started in with cocktails on the night of his secretary's birthday. That gave him a good start. He went out someplace to dinner and got loaded. He came back and got involved in a hit-and-run accident and didn't dare stop because he was drunk. So he made a clean getaway. But he'd smashed his car somewhat and he had to do something about that.

"He knew Vivian Deshler. My best guess is that Vivian had been involved in some other whiplash injury case, either herself or someone whom she knew pretty well. She knew that once the whiplash had been established, it was almost impossible for any doctor to give an accurate check on the injuries.

"So Holgate came to her as soon as he got sobered up enough to do some thinking. That was probably around midnight. He told her, 'Look, Vivian, I'm in a jam. Let me hit the rear end of your automobile. Then we'll fix up a synthetic time and a place where the accident happened, preferably sometime late in the afternoon but before I'd had my first cocktail. You can claim a whiplash injury and file a suit against me. I'll pretend that I don't know you, that you're a perfect stranger but I will shamefacedly admit liability. The insurance company will have to pay off. I'll get out of my jam on hit-and-run driving, you'll have a perfect whiplash injury case against the insurance company and—'"

Lamont Hawley snapped his fingers.

"It registers?" Sellers asked.

"You're damned right it registers," Hawley said. "Now I'm beginning to get the picture. By God, the guy's right!"

Sellers grinned. "Don't swear," he said, "ladies present."

"You're goddam right, ladies are present," Bertha said, "and let's cut out the horseplay. What do *you* know about all this, Hawley?"

"We don't *know*, but it begins to fit together," Hawley said. "We made a routine check to try and find witnesses to that crash and we couldn't find any. Of course, Holgate's story was straightforward and we didn't pay too much attention to that end of it. The thing that bothered us was the way the Vivian Deshler claim was made out. It had been made by some very shrewd attorney who knew all the ropes, or else by someone who had been— So *that's* it!"

I said to Bertha Cool, "Ask Elsie to come in here."

Bertha rang my office and Elsie Brand came in.

"How are your books on unsolved cases, Elsie?" I asked. "Do you have anything on hit-and-run cases within the last two or three months?"

"Lots of them," she said. "Volume G, classification two hundred. Do you want to see it?"

"I want to see it."

She looked at me apprehensively for a moment, then started for the door, turned, gave me a reassuring glance over her shoulder and was gone.

"What the hell are you doing, running a crime library?" Sellers asked.

"Something like that."

"He's putting in a hell of a lot of time on it," Bertha said. "That is, that moon-eyed secretary of his is."

"I don't get it," Sellers said, "unless you're trying to run competition with the police department."

I said nothing.

Sellers chewed on his cigar and said, "Of course, it could be bait. Whenever we catch you off first base, you try to tie in what you're doing with some case the police are interested in and want solved. We give you a lot of leeway because we think you may turn up with something we want. Come to think of it, you've pulled that trick in the last couple of cases."

Sellers' eyes narrowed. "You know, Lam," he said, "that's the trouble with you. You're a Pint-Size and it's awfully damned easy to underestimate you."

Elsie Brand was back, breathless with excitement and with the book under her arm.

"Here it is, Mr. Lam," she said, and bent over me. I could feel her breath on my cheek, her breast pressing against my shoulder.

She put the book on my lap and her left hand gave my arm a reassuring squeeze.

"Something about the thirteenth of August," I said. "Have you got them dated?"

Her nimble fingers turned the pages. "Here we are," she said.

"Was there a hit-and-run on August thirteenth?"

"Yes, yes. Right here!"

I looked at the clipping, then passed it over to Sergeant Sellers. "There you are, Sergeant," I said. "On the highway between Colinda and Los Angeles, a car weaving around the road sideswipes one car, goes out of control into a bus stop, kills two people and keeps going. All attempts to trace the car futile."

Sellers said, "*I'll* just ask a couple of questions. Elsie, you're this guy's secretary."

"Yes, sir."

"Was this scene rehearsed?"

"What do you mean?"

"Was it on the up and up? Did he play it straight? Had you told him about this hit-and-run before?"

"Oh, no, sir. I hadn't even noticed it before myself. I simply kept the scrapbooks."

Sellers turned to me. "You got any evidence that ties into this picture, Lam, or are you just playing it by ear and had a lucky break?"

"I have evidence that ties into it," I said. "The accident was supposed to be at three-thirty but I can produce a witness who will swear that Holgate's car was undamaged as late as four-thirty in the afternoon. This bus stop hit-and-run accident took place at six-twenty."

Sellers said, "That's not in my department, but I'll bet the traffic boys would sure as hell like to clear that one up. We don't like to have these hit-and-run drivers get away without being caught. It gives too much encouragement to drunk drivers."

Hawley said suddenly, "Here, wait a minute. Holgate is our client, Lam. He's covered with our company. You're getting us out of the frying pan into the fire."

"I don't make the facts," I said. "I uncover them."

Hawley said, "This is uncovering something we aren't going to like."

Sellers looked him over for a moment and said, "You wouldn't want to compound a felony, would you?"

"No, no, of course not."

"Well, if Lam is right about this thing, we'd better find out about it and you'd better give us all the cooperation necessary."

"Yes, Sergeant," Hawley said. "I was only commenting on an obvious aspect of the case."

"Well, don't comment on the obvious," Sellers said. "It isn't necessary." He looked at me and started chewing on his cigar.

"Well?" I asked.

"I just don't know about you," Sellers said. "Once you start talking, you charm the birds out of the trees and— Hell, I just don't know."

Sellers looked at the account again, then went over to Bertha Cool's telephone, picked it up, dialed a number, said,

"Sergeant Sellers talking. I want to speak with Captain Andover in Traffic."

A moment later he said, "Bill, this is Frank Sellers. I'm on the line of something that may clean up a hit-and-run accident that took place August thirteenth between Colinda and Los Angeles. A couple of people killed in a bus stop around six-twenty—drunk driver.

"Now, you got any witnesses that could give us any help there?"

Sellers listened for a while and said, "Now, don't get me wrong. I just said I was working on something that *might*, just possibly *might*, give us a lead on cleaning that up....Look, I'm going to drive around there after a while. I'll have someone with me. You get everything lined up."

Sellers hung up the phone, looked at me and shook his head. "Every time I think we've got you on the ropes, you come bobbing up behind me somewhere. Now dammit, Lam, if you're taking me for a ride on this thing. I'll...well, I'll give you something *you* won't forget in a hurry."

Sellers looked at his watch, looked over at Bertha and said, "I told an officer to have Chris Maxton, who's Holgate's partner, brought in here. Now, I'm going to have to leave before he gets here but when he comes I want you—"

The phone rang.

Bertha picked it up, said, "Hello," listened for a moment, then turned to Sellers and said, "They're here now."

"You have them come right on in," Sellers said. "We'll just take time to button up *this* angle before we go any farther."

Bertha said, "Send them in," and hung up the phone.

The door opened. One of the officers who had been at the airport stood on the threshold and said, "Come on in, Maxton."

The man who came in was the heavyset man I had met at

Elsie Brand's apartment, the one who had given me the two hundred and fifty dollars.

He looked at me, said, "You two-timing crook!" and started forward.

Sellers shoved out an expert foot and tripped him.

"Back into line, Buddy," Sellers said. "You don't like him? What's the matter?"

"Don't like him!" Maxton yelled. "The cheap crook! He took me for two hundred and fifty bucks."

"Tell us about it," Sellers said.

"There isn't anything much to tell," Maxton said. "My partner—"

"What's his name?"

"Carter Jackson Holgate."

"All right, go ahead."

"Well, my partner was involved in an automobile accident and I wanted to find some witnesses. I put an ad in the paper—"

"Use your name?" Sellers asked.

"No, it was just a box number."

"All right, go ahead."

"I put an ad in the paper offering two hundred and fifty dollars for a witness who had seen the accident. This cheap crook sent me a letter saying he had, and gave me a telephone number. He was supposed to be the brother of some woman named Elsie Brand, who has an apartment here in the city. He was supposed to be visiting her. He told a convincing enough story and I handed him two hundred and fifty bucks. Then I found out the accident didn't happen that way at all and he's a liar, he didn't see it."

Sellers looked at me.

"Why did you want a witness to the accident?" I asked.

"You know why. Because you always want witnesses to accidents."

"Your partner was insured?"

"Of course he was insured. It's partnership insurance. We wouldn't drive any of the cars without having insurance on them, public liability and property damage up to the limit."

"And your partner admitted that the accident was his fault?"

"Well, what if he did?"

"Well, why did you want witnesses?"

"I don't have to let you ask questions."

"And," I said, "after your first ad for a hundred dollars didn't bring forth a witness, your next ad ran for two hundred and fifty dollars."

Maxton turned and said to Sellers, "You're an officer?"

"That's right."

"All right, you seem to be in charge here," Maxton said. "I don't have to let this crook cross-examine me."

"Well, I'll ask you the same question myself," Sellers said. "Why did you increase the ante?"

"Because I wanted to find a witness."

"Why?"

"So there wouldn't be any question about what had happened."

"You knew the insurance company had hired a detective agency?"

"Hell, no. I was just trying to get things straightened out."

"Your partner know you put the ad in the paper?"

"Of course he— Well, I don't know that he knew, no. We pull together all the time. It was a close partnership, and Carter knew that I would help him in any way possible."

"You know where Holgate is now?" Sellers asked.

"No. He hasn't been in the office and police have been out there looking the place over. It was robbed last night but I don't think that had anything to do with this— Or did it?"

Maxton whirled to look at me.

Sellers jerked his thumb at the officer and said, "Take him out. Don't tell him anything for a while."

"Say, what's all this about?" Maxton asked. "What— I came up here to prosecute a crook for obtaining money under false pretenses. You're acting as though I might be charged with something."

Sellers simply jerked his thumb at the officer.

"This way," the officer said to Maxton, and took him by the arm.

Maxton started to hold back. The officer increased the pressure and Maxton went out.

Sellers chewed on his cigar.

"This is the damnedest case," Hawley said irritably.

Sellers said, "Come on, Pint Size. We're going places."

10

Captain William Andover of Traffic went with us to call on Mrs. Eloise Troy. He said she was the only witness whose testimony would be worth anything in connection with that hit-run traffic accident.

Sellers said to Andover, "Would it be all right if I did the questioning, Bill? I'm working on something a lot bigger than this traffic. I'm working on a murder case."

"Go right ahead," Captain Andover said. "I'm working on a hot lead in this case, but I'm not ready to tip my hand yet. You go ahead."

Sergeant Sellers rang the bell.

Mrs. Eloise Troy turned out to be a straightforward, rather fleshy widow, around fifty-two or fifty-three. She wore glasses, seemed poised and sensible.

Captain Andover identified himself and introduced us.

"We wanted to talk about that hit-run accident last August," Sellers said.

"Heavens, I've told everything I know about that half a dozen times."

"Would you mind going over it just once more?" Sellers said, "because I want to hear it first hand. I'm working on a lead which just might pan out."

"Well, I certainly hope it does," she said. "That was the most callous, brutal thing I have ever seen. It just made me sick to my stomach. I couldn't sleep for a long while without having nightmares about what happened."

"Would you mind telling us?"

"I can go over it again all right," she said. "Come in and sit down."

Her flat was a comfortable, homey place, with the aroma of good cooking coming from the kitchen.

She closed the kitchen door and said, "I'm cooking some chicken in a rotisserie and it gives a perfectly ravishing aroma, but very penetrating. I wasn't expecting company."

"It's all right, we'll only be a minute," Sellers said.

"Oh, I don't mind that at all. I just thought the flat was a little, well a little odoriferous."

We took chairs and Mrs. Troy said, "Well, it was about six-thirty in the afternoon, I guess, right after the rush hour. I was driving toward Los Angeles and this car was coming behind me.

"I always make it a point to look at my rearview mirror from time to time, just to keep a line on what's coming behind. Driving in traffic, if you have to stop, it always makes a great deal of difference about the car that's right behind you. You want to know whether it's a driver who has his car under control or whether he's one that might bang into the rear end.

"Heaven knows, I've had *that* happen."

Sellers nodded sympathetically.

"Well, I saw this car quite a ways back and the man was drunk. Now, there's no question about that. The man was drunk."

"Could you describe the car?"

"Now, that is the thing I can't do," she said. "I can tell you that it was a big car, a dark car, a modern, shiny car—you know, it wasn't an old beat-up model. It was new and it was a pretty big car."

"He was weaving around?" Sellers asked.

"I'll say he was. He almost sideswiped a car as he went

around it, and then he cut in on another car and crowded it clean off the road and then I just said to myself, Heavens, that man is drunk and the Lord knows what he's going to do. I'm going to slow down and get over to the side of the road.

"So I slowed and got over to the side of the road and he just came tearing along right up behind me and I thought he was going to run right into my rear end. Then he swerved out abruptly, swerved too far and then swung back. The hind end of his car just sideswiped the front part of mine, and that seemed to put him entirely out of control. He swung over way to the left and then back to the right and went right through this group of people who were waiting for the bus."

"You didn't get his license number or anything?" Sellers asked.

"Heavens, no. I was too busy fighting my own car trying to get it stopped and keep it under control. He hit the front end and pushed it off the side of the road and then when I tried to get back, the shoulder of the highway jerked on my steering wheel and I had to stop—and I guess I was shaken up a bit."

"You don't need to say anything about that," Captain Andover said. "In case you ever have to give your testimony, Mrs. Troy, don't say anything about being shaken up because some lawyer would grab hold of that and make it appear you were too hysterical to know what you were talking about."

"I wasn't hysterical," she said. "I was shaken up a bit and I was annoyed and…well, I certainly wasn't hysterical—not what I'd call hysterical."

"You don't know anything about this car, what kind it was, other than that it was big?"

"That's all."

"And he sideswiped your car?"

"Yes."

Captain Andover said, "We took the paint that had been rubbed on her fender and gave it a microscopic examination and a spectroscopic examination. It came from a late model Buick."

"That's Holgate's car," I said. "That is, his was a late model Buick."

Sellers' eyes narrowed. "Did you get anything—any look at the car that would give you a clue? Just think carefully. Was there anything about the car—anything that seemed distinctive?"

"No," she said. "I can't remember so much about the car. I did get a good look at the driver."

Sellers straightened. "You got a good look at *him*?"

"Yes."

"What can you tell about him?"

"Well, he looked sort of…well, he was a big man with a western hat and he had a mustache, I remember that, one of these close-clipped mustaches and he was wearing one of these sort of whipcord suits. You know, the kind that officers and cowboys and some forest rangers and outdoor people wear."

Sellers and Andover exchanged glances.

"Do you think you'd know his picture if you saw it?" Sellers asked.

"Well, I don't know. It's awfully hard to identify people from pictures. Perhaps if I saw a profile I might."

"Suppose you looked at the man, do you think you could identify him?"

"I think I could. His appearance is etched on my mind."

Sellers said, "This may come as a shock to you, Mrs. Troy, but we have a man we'd like to have you look at. Now, this man is—well, frankly, he's in the morgue. Now that would be something of a shock, but it would be very much in the interests of justice if you'd take a look."

"Dead people don't bother me," she said. "I'll look."

Sellers took a photograph from his pocket and said, "Now, I'm going to show you a photograph of a man's profile. I don't want you to let this photograph influence you. If you can identify it, all right. If you can't, I don't want you to look at the dead man and just because you've seen his photograph think that's the man you saw."

"I understand."

Sellers handed her a profile photograph.

She looked at it and said, "Why...why, yes...I *think* that's the man. It looks like him."

Sellers took the picture away from her, put it back in his pocket and said, "I think you're going to have to accompany us to the morgue, Mrs. Troy, if you don't mind. It'll only be a short trip. We'll take you there and then we'll have an officer bring you right back home."

"I don't mind. When do you want me to go?"

"Right now—that is, just as soon as you can."

"Well, heavens; I've got this chicken in the rotisserie and—"

"Isn't there some neighbor you could ask to look at it for you?" Sellers asked.

"Oh," she said, "it isn't *that* important. I'll shut it off. It won't affect the flavor too much. I'll just shut off the current and turn it on when I come back. We won't be long, will we?"

"Not too long," Sellers said.

She said, "You just give me a minute."

She bustled into the kitchen and Sellers and Andover exchanged glances.

"I sure as hell would like to button this one up," Andover said.

Sellers looked at me. "You lucky sonofabitch! If you can squirm out of *this* one, you sure as hell *are* ringed with luck."

"I'm not squirming out of anything," I told him. "I'm simply giving you the breaks, that's all."

"*You're* giving *me* the breaks!" Sellers said. He shook his head. "That's more typical of you than anything you could have said. *You're* giving *us* the breaks."

We drove to the morgue. The two officers sat in front. Mrs. Troy sat in back with me.

"What's your interest in this, Mr. Lam?" she asked.

"Lam's a detective," Sellers said over his shoulder, "and while he appreciates everything you're doing, he doesn't want to discuss what he has in mind."

"Oh, I understand, I understand," Mrs. Troy said. "I was just asking to be polite."

"Well, you know how it is in this business," Sellers said. "We have to be pretty closemouthed."

"Oh, I understand I'm sure. You don't have to make any explanations to me."

She didn't ask any more questions.

We got to the morgue and Sellers said, "You wait out here in the car, Pint Size. We'll do this without your fine Italian hand gumming up the works."

They were inside about fifteen minutes. When they came out Sellers was shaking his head.

"Okay," I said, "what happened?"

"What happened?" Sellers said. "You know what happened. She made an identification—not a one-hundred percent positive identification, but an identification all right.

"She took a look at the mustache from the side and said she knows that's the man because of the mustache—and of course you know what some attorney would do on cross-examination. He'd claim she didn't identify the man, she identified the mustache. But it's an identification, all right.

"She says the man was drunk and his eyes were sort of what she calls droopy and heavy-lidded and he was sort of slouched over the steering wheel, but she got a look at his face all right and she remembers about the mustache. Of course, Pint Size, between you and me, a goddam mustache has accounted for more mistaken identifications than anything the world has ever known. But, nevertheless, she made an identification—a pretty damned positive identification."

"We're driving her back?" I asked.

"We are not," Sellers said. "We're sending her back home with an officer and by God, if I catch you trying to talk with her and influence her testimony in any way. I'll slap you in a dungeon where you won't know whether it's day or night, and where you'll be living on bread and water for thirty days. I get so damned fed up with you stepping in and masterminding my cases, that it's hard for me to keep my hands off you.

"We fool around with a lot of methodical police work and solve our cases by good, hard intensive work and you come along with some hocus-pocus and pull a rabbit out of the hat."

"And I take it," I said, "that now we are going to look up Vivian Deshler."

"What a genius!" Sellers exclaimed sarcastically. "Now, who would ever have thought of that? That's sheer genius, Lam. Here we have two parties testifying to an automobile accident and you come along with the bright idea that the accident never happened, that it was a cover-up for a hit-and-run, and we get a witness who indicates that you're right. And then you surmise or deduce that we're going to talk with the other party involved in the accident.

"Now, isn't that just *too* clever?"

"You don't need to be so damned sarcastic," I told him. "As Mrs. Troy said, I was just trying to be polite."

"Well, you don't need to bother," Sellers said, biting down on his soggy cigar.

"I notice it doesn't cramp your style any," I told him.

"What doesn't?"

"Trying to be polite."

"You're damned right it doesn't," Sellers said. "Hang on, Pint Size, we're going to interview Vivian Deshler before some cooperative sonofabitch gets the word to her and she starts clamming up or consulting an attorney."

11

Vivian Deshler came to the door in response to our ring, opened it a crack, looked out and saw Frank Sellers. "Oh, how do you do, Sergeant?" she said. "My heavens, I'm dressing and— Well, Donald, too! Is everything straightened out all right?"

"We'd like to come in and talk with you for a minute," Sellers said.

"Well, I'm sorry. I'm just not presentable, that's all. I…I'm dressing."

"Haven't you got a robe?" Sellers asked.

"I have it on."

"Well, then, what's holding you back?" Sellers said. "Open the door. We just want to talk for a minute."

"I'm hardly presentable."

"We're not trying to judge a beauty contest," Sellers told her. "We're trying to clean up a murder case."

She pouted a bit and said, "I like to look my best when good-looking men are calling on me, but…well, come in." She opened the door.

We went in and Sellers jerked his cold cigar toward a chair. "Sit down," he said. "We'll only be a minute."

She seated herself, and the robe slid smoothly back along one bare leg. She gave a little kittenish gesture, retrieved the robe and pulled it back over the flesh.

"See what I mean?" she said.

"What?" Sellers asked.

"About not being dressed."

"I don't get it," Sellers said.

She started to say something, then looked at me and smiled. "Donald got it," she said.

"All right," Sellers said, "let's quit beating around the bush. I want to know about that automobile accident."

"Heavens, not again! I've told that so many times."

"What time?" Sellers asked.

"Now, I can't be absolutely certain about the time," she said, with her eyes downcast and counting on her fingers with her thumb. "It was along in the afternoon and it might have been... well, now I just don't know. I've been trying to think back on what happened that day and I can't remember exactly the time. You see, Sergeant, I was pretty well shaken up and I didn't realize at the time I'd been seriously hurt. I started driving to my apartment and then somewhere along the line I guess I blacked out. The next thing I knew I was in my apartment and then everything went blank and— Well, of course by that time I knew I was shaken up and injured but I certainly didn't think it was anything real *serious*. I thought I was just excited and— Well, I've read about fainting spells and what can happen from an emotional shock and I thought that's what I was experiencing."

Sellers said, "All right, I'm going to put it to you cold turkey. Was there an automobile accident?"

"Was there an automobile accident?" she echoed. "Why, *what* in the world do you mean? Of course there was."

"I want to know just this," Sellers said. "Did Holgate run into the back of your car or is it a cover-up?"

"What do you mean, a cover-up?"

Sellers said, "There's evidence that Holgate was mixed up in a hit-and-run deal and had the front end of his car smashed in, that you and Holgate cooked up a deal by which he could account for his smashed front end on the car and you could help him out and present a claim to the insurance company for—"

"What in the world *are* you talking about? The accident took place just as I have described it. I wouldn't try to defraud any insurance company and I had never met Mr. Holgate prior to the time that he ran into the rear of my automobile and we exchanged names from our driving licenses."

Sellers looked at me thoughtfully. "Want to ask any questions, Pint Size?"

I said, "Who prepared the claim you submitted to the insurance company, Miss Deshler?"

She regarded me with a head-to-toe sweep of the eyes and her manner suddenly changed. "That," she said, "doesn't have anything to do with the accident or anything else. In short, it's none of your business, Mr. Lam."

I said, "I'll ask you one other question. Have you ever been in an automobile accident before?"

She looked at Frank Sellers and said, "Do I have to sit here and submit to this kind of questioning? After all, you're trying to solve a murder case. What difference does it make if I'd been in a thousand automobile accidents?"

"He was just asking," Sellers said.

"Well, I'm just answering," she snapped. "It's none of his business. And now, gentlemen, I don't have all afternoon to sit around here in my underwear and swap words with you. I've got to get busy and dress. I'm going out tonight. I've had a hard day and I want to look my best when I go out."

Sellers said, "We're not making any accusations but you know things *could* get awfully sticky if you started playing tag in a murder case. Now I'm going to ask you this: Did you hire a detective agency to do anything?"

"Heavens, no."

"To keep tabs on Lamont Hawley, the agent of the Consolidated Interinsurance Company?"

"No, I told you. No, no, no! Ten thousand times no! I didn't hire any detective agency, period. Now will you people *please* get out of here."

The telephone rang.

She crossed over to the instrument to pick it up and answer it. She didn't bother about her robe, which fell open to show she was wearing a bra and panties.

Sellers looked her over, looked at me and said, "You want to try any more questioning?"

"Of course," I said. "You haven't skimmed the surface yet. What did you think she was going to do, break down and tell you, yes, I worked this thing out in order to defraud the insurance company and it led to murder? Do *you* usually get confessions that easy?"

Sellers said, "There's something about this thing that doesn't ring true to me. I don't like it. We're skating on thin ice."

She said, "This is a telephone call for you, Sergeant Sellers. It's from a Captain Andover in Traffic. Says he has to speak to you right away on a matter of the greatest importance."

Sellers went over, picked up the telephone, shifted the cigar over to the other side of his mouth, said, "Yeah? Sellers speaking....Shoot."

He was silent for a minute, then said, "What the hell!"

Again there was more conversation.

Vivian Deshler started looking at me, sizing me up, then managed to smile and said, "I hope you come out all right, Donald."

She shifted her position again and again the robe slid down her bare leg. She reached for it coyly, pulled it back and said, "I can sympathize with you. If there's anything I can do—legitimately..."

Sergeant Sellers slammed up the telephone, said, "Okay, Pint Size, on our way."

I said, "I'd like to finish—"

"On our way."

Sellers turned around to Vivian Deshler and said, "I'm awfully sorry we came barging in here this way, Miss Deshler, but it was on a matter that was quite important and I had to check on it—and we have quite a time working against a schedule and all that."

"It's all right, Sergeant," she said. "It was a pleasure. If you folks will come again sometime when I'm not caught completely unawares. I'll buy you a drink."

I said, "I want to ask a couple more questions, and—"

Sergeant Sellers took my arm and literally pushed me out the door.

She gave us a parting smile and then the door closed behind her.

"You and your theories," Sellers said.

"What's the matter now?" I asked.

"I told you about mustaches," Sellers said. "Dammit, if I was wearing a mustache I'd shave the thing off before I even got in the automobile. I'd cut it off with a jackknife if I had to. I don't think I'd even wait long enough to get to a barbershop."

"What's eating you now?" I asked.

"Mistaken identification."

"Who?"

"That Troy woman."

"What about her?"

"Andover told me he'd been working on a lead that was pretty much undercover. You remember that? He said he didn't want to take a chance on wrecking it by showing his hand prematurely, but after this identification by Mrs. Troy he decided he might just as well shoot the works, so he started running this thing down and what do you know?"

"I don't know anything," I said irritably. "What do you know?"

"Well," Sellers said, "for your information, Pint Size, the automobile that killed those two people wasn't driven by Carter Holgate at all. It was driven by a man named Swanton, who was driving a big late model Buick and had got himself pretty well loaded at a cocktail party. His car wasn't damaged very much and he thought he'd got the whole thing covered up and was sitting pretty, but when we got that identification on Holgate, Andover thought he'd better go talk with this guy and put the cards on the table."

"What happened?" I asked.

"What happened?" Sellers said. "The guy caved. He'd had his conscience gnawing on him for quite a while, and the minute Andover made a pass at him the guy broke down and admitted the whole damned business, started wringing his hands and telling how sorry he was and what this was going to mean to his family, and how he didn't know how in the world he had ever done a thing like that; that it was foreign to his nature, that he didn't realize how drunk he was, that he couldn't think straight, that— Hell, all the rest of it."

"Is there any resemblance to Holgate?" I asked.

"Quite a striking resemblance," Andover said. "Both of them are big men with mustaches and this guy wears Texas hats and whipcord suits—so there's your high-powered theory that you had me running around on all shot to hell.

"You know, Donald, if you child geniuses would just mind your own goddam business and let us officers run the police department according to the accepted theories of systematic investigation, you'd save yourself a lot of trouble and perhaps in the course of time I could learn to overcome that feeling of irritation which grips me every time you stick your neck out with one of these theories of yours.

"Come on now, we're going back to headquarters."

"Can I make one more suggestion?" I asked.

"No," he said and his voice had a hard crack to it. "I've finished listening to you and your theories. You're a prime suspect in a murder case. We're going back to headquarters and if the deputy district attorney says okay, you're going into the felony tank and you aren't going to talk your way out from nothing."

I said, "I don't know what kind of a pull the Ace High people have with you, but I'd like to find out. What do they do, send you a case of cigars every Christmas?"

"What the hell are you talking about?" he asked.

I said, "The Ace High Detective Agency was mixed in this thing and you're certainly letting them off the hook. If it had been Cool and Lam, you'd have had us on the grid and—"

"Oh, forget it," he said. "You've got a persecution complex."

"Probably I have," I told him, "but this much is certain. The Ace High was investigating Holgate and probably investigating that accident. Heaven knows what they've found out and they certainly aren't going to pick up the telephone and tell you.

"You go ahead and play it real cozy with them if you want to. The next time you want information out of us—"

Sellers clamped down on his cigar angrily for a moment, then said, "Listen, Pint Size, did it ever occur to you there isn't going to be any next time? You're going to be charged with murder within the next forty-eight hours and you're going to have one hell of a time trying to beat the rap.

"I'll admit there are some things in the case that are a little cockeyed but we'll get them all buttoned up before we get done. Personally, I don't think you killed him, but you certainly stuck your neck out in such a way that you became a prize patsy, and I don't think you're going to be able to convince a jury you're such a sweet, innocent little lamb."

Sellers thought for a minute and then grinned and said, "And that's not a bad pun, in case you're interested."

I said, "It's okay by me. Just remember that I told you the Ace High had been investigating Holgate and the accident and that you did nothing about it."

"Now, wait a minute. What's the idea of that crack?"

"I've given you warning," I said. "When I put on my defense I'll make a real issue out of that. There'll be no holds barred."

Sellers said, "In other words you'd try to make something out of the fact that I didn't— Oh, hell, it's all right with me. The city's paying for my gasoline. If you want to make a trip to the Ace High people, we'll make a trip to the Ace High people and then you won't have *anything* to squawk about."

I settled back against the cushions and said, "I'd just like to see how soft you are with some of the other agencies."

"You'll see," he said grimly.

12

Morley Patton, the manager of the Ace High Detective Agency, regarded us with something less than cordiality.

"This is official business," Sellers said.

"And so you bring one of my competitors along with you to listen?" Patton asked.

"Now, don't be that way," Sellers told him. "I'm running this thing and I have to have Lam here because there are certain things about the case he knows."

"And probably a lot of other things he'd like to know," Patton said.

"All right, you had a tail on Donald Lam," Sellers said. "How did it happen?"

"I don't think we have to discuss that and I'm not admitting that we had a tail on Lam."

I said, "Put it this way, Patton. You were shadowing a Doris Ashley at the Miramar Apartments in Colinda and when I entered the picture and got acquainted with her, you put a tail on me."

"I don't have to answer *your* questions, that's a cinch," Patton said.

"All right," Sellers said, his face darkening, "you're going to have to answer mine. Now did you have a tail on Doris Ashley or not?"

"It depends on what you mean by—"

"You know what I mean," Sellers said. "Now, you can answer that question yes or no and damned fast."

"Yes," Patton said.

"You were keeping her car at her apartment under surveillance?" I asked.

"You're talking to my deaf ear," Patton said.

"Were you?" Sellers asked. "I'll make it *my* question and put it to the other ear."

Patton said, "Yes."

"All right, who was your client?"

"We don't have to tell you that."

"I think you do."

"I don't."

"For your information," Sellers said, "this is now being tied into a murder case."

"Murder!" Patton exclaimed.

"You heard me."

"Who was murdered?"

"Carter Holgate. Know anything about him?"

"He...he enters into the picture in a general way," Patton said, choosing his words cautiously now, and his manner showing that he was apprehensive.

"All right," Sellers said, "I think the identity of your client may have something to do with our investigation. I want to know who was employing you."

"Just a minute," Patton said, "let me get the record."

He walked over to a filing case, pulled out a jacket, opened it, looked at some papers, dropped the jacket back into the file and stood frowning.

"We're waiting," Sellers said. "And for your information, the police like a little more active cooperation from a private detective agency in connection with a murder case."

"How much cooperation are Cool and Lam giving you?" Patton asked.

"All I'm asking for," Sellers said. And then added with a grin, "More than I'm asking for."

"Well, I'll tell you this," Patton said. "Our client was just a telephone number in Salt Lake City. Money for our services was received in the form of cash and we were instructed to telephone developments as fast as they happened to whoever might answer at this number."

"And you didn't look up the number?" Sellers asked.

"Sure, we looked it up," Patton said. "We're not that naïve. It was the number of an apartment that was rented to a man named Oscar Bowman. It was a hotel apartment. No one knew anything about Bowman. He had paid the rent for a month in advance and that was it. Sometimes a man's voice answered the telephone when we phoned in for instructions and sometimes a woman's voice.

"We had Doris Ashley under surveillance for about a week. That is, we kept her apartment under surveillance, or rather her car at the apartment house. When she'd come out or go in, we'd clock the times of arrival and departure.

"When Lam showed an interest in the picture, we reported on that, and when Lam had made a contact and gone up to her apartment house with her, we phoned in that information and were instructed to drop the whole thing, to mail a report and terminate our activities at once."

"You mailed the report to the apartment in Salt Lake?" Sellers asked.

"No, we didn't. We mailed the report to Oscar Bowman, General Delivery, Colinda."

"The hell," Sellers said. "What about your fees?"

"We had received a retainer in the form of cash in an envelope sent through the mail. There is still a credit to the client on the case. We were instructed to forget about the credit and close out the case."

"In other words," Sellers said, "when Lam got on the job, it caused them to press the panic button and get out?"

"I don't know," Patton said. "All I know is what happened. I'm telling that to you."

"Who told you to close up the case when you telephoned? Was it a man or a woman that was talking?"

"I remember that very distinctly. It was a woman talking."

I said, "On a deal of that sort, Sergeant, they'd protect themselves."

"What do you mean?"

"He'd tell her to hang on for a minute and he'd switch the phone conversation onto a recording. They've got a recording of the thing somewhere."

Sellers looked at Patton.

Patton said to me, "I wish you'd drop dead."

"He will someday," Sellers said, "but right now I'm interested in finding out whether you have a recording of that conversation."

"We have a recording."

"Let's listen."

"*You* can listen," Patton said, "if you get tough about it. Lam can't listen. We don't have to turn the records of our employment over to a competitive agency, particularly when that man figures in the case and—"

"You're right," Sellers said. "I'm going to get tough about it. And I'm beginning to do a little thinking on my own.

"Donald, you can just toddle along. I know where to get you whenever I want you. Don't try to pull any fast ones. Don't try to leave town."

Patton's face lit up. "You mean he's a suspect?"

"I mean he's a suspect," Sellers said, "and before I get done prowling through your records, there's just a chance little Pint

Size here is going to find himself mixed up in that murder worse than ever."

Patton became downright cordial. "If you'll step right this way, Sergeant," he said, "I'll dig out the records of the conversation. For your information, the whole conversation was recorded. That is, we phoned a report on Donald Lam entering the picture and immediately were ordered to discontinue our surveillance and close up the case, to send a final report to Oscar Bowman, care of General Delivery, Colinda and to keep the credit, whatever it might be....It's all recorded on tape."

Sellers took the cigar out of his mouth. "Get lost, Pint Size," he said to me. "I'll get in touch with you when I want you—and that may be pretty damned soon. If you've got any business you want to wind up, you'd better wind it up."

I took a taxi to the offices of Cool & Lam, went up in the elevator, pushed my way through the big glass door into the reception room, nodded to the girl at the switchboard and said, "Don't bother to tell Bertha I'm here for a minute. I want to—"

"But she wanted to know in case you came in, Mr. Lam. She wanted you *just* as soon as you arrived."

"All right," I said. "Tell her I'm on my way in."

I walked through the door marked B. COOL — PRIVATE. Bertha was just hanging up the phone.

"All right, Donald," she said. "What happened?"

I said, "They jerked the rug out from under me. The bottom fell out."

"What happened to all this theory of yours?"

"Out the window. Down the drain," I said. "It was nice while it lasted."

"It's no good?"

"No good."

"Where does that leave you?"

"Behind the eight ball."

"What's Sellers doing?"

"Getting an earful from the Ace High Detective Agency."

"An earful or an eyeful?"

"Both. They have some recorded telephone conversations he's listening to. Whoever it was hired them got in a panic as soon as it appeared another detective agency was interested and ordered the investigation stopped and the case closed out."

"Why?"

"That," I said, "is what I've got to figure out."

"You've been figuring out too damned much," Bertha said. "You got a theory and tried to sell Sellers on it and when the theory busted it leaves you behind the eight ball. If you'd just sat tight and told him it was up to the police to prove their case, it wouldn't have looked so bad for you.

"How in hell do they figure you could have picked up Holgate's body and shoved it into the trunk of the agency automobile?"

"They figure I might have had an accomplice," I said. "Those things do happen."

"Phooey!" Bertha said. "It would take an accomplice that was strong as an ox and— Who the hell would be so involved as to get mixed up in murder with you?"

I looked her straight in the eyes. "You."

"Me!" Bertha screamed.

"You," I said.

"What in hell are you talking about?"

I said, "I'm talking about police thinking. After they get done manufacturing a case against me and looking for an accomplice that would stand by me in a murder, someone who was sufficiently interested to go all the way in the thing, they'll start thinking about you."

"Fry me for an oyster!" Bertha said.

"They may do just that," I told her.

Bertha said, "How do you know this Mrs. Troy isn't lying? She may—"

"She is lying," I said. "They've got the party who killed those two people at the bus stop. It wasn't Holgate at all. Mrs. Troy made a mistaken identification. She didn't identify a man, she identified a mustache and some western clothes."

Bertha's diamonds glittered as her pudgy fingers started drumming on the top of the desk.

"Of all the damned cases!" she said.

That gave me a grin. I said, "This is one that *you* picked, remember? You wanted one of the nice, quiet, respectable kind of cases. You were tired of the spectacular hairbreadth escape cases that I dreamed up."

"Where's Sellers now?" she asked.

"At the Ace High."

"You get the hell down to your office," she said, "and you let me talk with Sellers. If he comes messing in here with any of his accomplice theories, I'll pin his ears back, but good."

"Remember," I told her, "that anything you say may be used against you."

I looked back as I went out the door. She was sitting there with her mouth open, so damned mad she was temporarily speechless.

Elsie Brand was waiting for me in my office. "Did it pan out, Donald?" she asked eagerly.

I shook my head. "It didn't pan out," I said, "and dammit, it should have. Everything would have fitted in nicely but—"

"Why didn't it pan out? I thought—"

"It didn't pan out because a fellow by the name of Swanton had his conscience bothering him and the minute the police pointed a finger at him, he started confessing all over the place."

"You mean to the murder?"

"No, no. To the hit-and-run. You can cross that off your books now. That's solved."

"Oh, Donald," she said. "I'm so sorry."

Her eyes were sympathetic. She seemed almost on the point of tears.

I said, "Well, there's no use wasting sympathy at this point, Elsie. We've just got to start thinking constructively."

"Can I help?" she asked, her voice showing that she wanted to help, that she desperately wanted to help.

"I don't know," I told her.

"Of course, Donald, you asked for the hit-and-run accidents on the evening of the thirteenth and as soon as I told you about that one in the bus stop you grabbed on it, but actually there were two and—"

I looked at her for a moment, then suddenly jerked her up out of the chair, put my arms around her and started dancing around the office.

"Donald!" she exclaimed. "What in the world are you doing?"

"Sweetheart," I said, "I love you. I—"

"Oh, Donald!"

"Why in hell didn't you take a chair and club me over the head when you saw me pulling a bonehead like that?"

"A bonehead like what?"

"Taking one case and not asking if there were any more. Quick, Elsie, what's the other one?"

"This one was written up as kind of a gag," she said. "It doesn't amount to much but it was a hit-and-run and—"

"Where is it, where is it?" I asked. "Come on, quick. Give."

She said, "This, of all things, is the chief of police of Colinda. Someone sideswiped his car, knocked it into the ditch and then kept right on going."

"The chief of police of Colinda," I said. "How nice. What's his name?"

"Let's see," she said. "It's a funny name for a police officer. I'll look it up. It's more like the name of a movie star. It's— Wait a minute, it's Montague A. Dale. You understand, Donald, it wasn't his private car, it was the city's car, the one they furnish the chief and—well, it seems that the thing happened so suddenly Chief Dale was busy trying to keep his car from upsetting and didn't get a good look at the car that went past other than it was a big car, and I believe he said he thought it was a Buick. But he didn't get the license number, and the city council was inclined to be a little sarcastic about—"

"Darling," I said, "never mind any more. Did that happen on the thirteenth?"

"On the thirteenth," she said.

"And at what time?"

"At five-thirty."

I pulled her to me and kissed her. "Elsie," I said, "you're a dear. You're a lifesaver. You're the sweetest thing ever invented. You're a combination of molasses, sugar, saccharin and honey. If anybody wants me, tell them to go to hell."

I went tearing out of the office.

13

I got in touch with Montague Dale just as he was closing up his office for the evening, and he wasn't in too good a mood.

"It'll have to be brief, Lam," he said when I gave him my card. "I'm late now. I've been working in connection with that Holgate case, and my wife is having some friends in for cocktails and dinner. I'm late and you know what happens when a man's late for an outfit of that sort.

"Moreover, I understand from the sheriff's office and the Los Angeles police that *you're* mixed up in this Holgate case in a big way and I guess it's my duty to warn you that anything you say can be used against you. Now, I don't have any personal hard feelings. Thank heavens, the Holgate case is out of my jurisdiction because it's beyond the city limits of Colinda. It's in the hands of the sheriff and the metropolitan police in Los Angeles. On account of the conditions under which the body was found—apparently nobody knows just where the guy was murdered.

"Now then, what's on your mind?"

I said, "This doesn't have anything to do with the Holgate case—at least, not directly."

"All right, what is it?"

I said, "Your car was sideswiped a while back and you were run into the ditch and—"

His face suddenly purpled. He said, "Now look, Lam, I've discussed that all I want to, and there's no need trying to needle me...."

"I think I can perhaps help you solve that accident," I said.

He stared at me. "You think you can find who did it?"

"I think *you* can find who did it," I said. "*I* give *you* a clue."

His face suddenly relaxed. He went over to his office desk, picked up the phone, dialed a number and said, "Hello, darling. An emergency has just come up....Yes, yes, I know....You carry on. I may be just a little bit late....All right, honey, that's the way it goes."

He hung up the telephone, gestured toward a chair and said, "Sit down, Lam. Sit down and make yourself comfortable. Now tell me about it."

I said, "I'm going to put the cards right on the table with you, Chief."

"That's the best way to do. Go ahead."

I said, "I have an idea about what happened on the thirteenth of August. I've tried to sell that idea to the Los Angeles police. Sergeant Sellers investigated it with me and we thought we'd struck pay dirt. Then the thing blew up in our faces and he's off me. He's off the whole theory."

"Well, if it blew up in his face, you can't blame him."

I said, "Only one phase of it did. We got hold of the wrong phase. We took the wrong turn in the road."

"All right, what's the right turn in the road?"

"You are."

He said, "Don't talk in circles, Lam. Put it on the table."

I said, "All right. Holgate had an automobile accident on the thirteenth of August. He reported to the insurance company that he had collided with the rear of an automobile driven by Vivian Deshler who lives at the Miramar Apartments and that the accident was his fault. The front end of his car was caved in, not so bad that he couldn't drive it, but nevertheless caved in, and the injuries to Vivian Deshler's car were rather slight."

Chief Dale's eyes narrowed. "Go on," he said.

I said, "Vivian Deshler said she had sustained a whiplash injury and made a claim against the insurance company. From the way the claim was prepared the insurance company felt there was a professional hand somewhere in the background."

"A shrewd lawyer?"

"Could have been."

"Go on, Lam."

"Well, the funny thing is that there were no witnesses to the accident, that the front end of Holgate's automobile was pretty badly caved in, but the back of Vivian Deshler's car, which was a light car and should have been the one that sustained the most damage, was only slightly injured.

"There were some other things about the accident that began to look a little peculiar. Then I found out that Holgate's car apparently was in good condition at four-thirty on the afternoon of the thirteenth; yet the accident was supposed to have taken place about three-thirty. I guess there's no question that Vivian Deshler's automobile was damaged by three-thirty in the afternoon. Doris Ashley, her friend, saw the car at that time and the tail end had been crumpled—not too bad but enough to notice."

"Go on," Dale said.

I said, "The records show that nobody said anything about any accident taking place at the location given in Colinda until the next day.

"Now then, under all the circumstances it occurred to me that perhaps Holgate had been mixed up in a hit-and-run accident that happened sometime in the evening, that he was in a quandary as to what to do; that he told his girlfriend, Vivian Deshler, about it, and Vivian Deshler said, 'Well, my car was damaged this afternoon. Why don't we claim that the damage

to your car was done when it hit my car and report it as an automobile accident?'

"'That would account for the damages to your car. You could
take it right in and have it fixed. You could report an accident to
the insurance company. They'd have an appraiser come and
take a look at your car and then the claim agent would come
and talk with me and I'd tell him my story. That would account
for the damages to your car and let you out of the hit-and-run
deal.'"

A smile began to spread across the chief's face. "You got anything that'll support this except theory?" he asked.

I said, "I think we can get quite a bit. If Holgate's car wasn't
smashed at four-thirty in the afternoon, if Vivian Deshler's car
was smashed at three-thirty, that's pretty damned good evidence that the report of the accident was a fake."

"Would Holgate get murdered on account of it?"

"I don't know," I said. "I don't think that Holgate contem-
plated the fact that his girlfriend, Vivian Deshler, was going to
put in a whopping big claim against the insurance company for a
whiplash injury. I think that the minute that happened, Holgate
realized he was involved in a criminal conspiracy, in obtaining
money under false pretenses, that he could go to prison, and
that he'd got himself out of the frying pan and into the fire.
I think perhaps Holgate began to get cold feet and wanted to
get out.

"I think that when Holgate realized the insurance company
wasn't satisfied with the explanation he had made about how
the accident occurred, he became terribly apprehensive, and
since a chain is no stronger than its weakest link, the people
who were mixed in it with him—"

"You mean Vivian Deshler murdered him in order to keep
him from blabbing?"

"I don't know who murdered him," I said. "The murder may have no connection with the hit-and-run accident. On the other hand, it may all be tied in together.

"What I'm doing is tying up loose ends, and what you're interested in is getting this hit-and-run accident solved."

"Am *I* interested in it!" he said. "That's the understatement of the year. That damned hit-and-run may cost me my job if I can't solve it."

"Mind telling me about it?" I asked.

"Hell, no," he said. "I was driving along the street going home when I saw this car coming behind me and I didn't like the way it was driving. It didn't occur to me that the man was drunk but I thought it was reckless driving. I pulled off to the side of the road and just as the man came up I held out my arm for him to stop. I was going to flag him down, take a look at his license, throw a scare into him and maybe give him a ticket.

"Instead of doing what he should have done, he swerved the car directly toward me, smashed into the left rear of my car, pushed me clean over into the ditch. Then his car glanced off and away he went.

"I was shoved off the road so far I thought I was going over. I was fighting the steering wheel for a matter of seconds. My left rear tire had blown out under the impact. I couldn't chase him and under the circumstances I didn't get any kind of a description.

"It's one of those things. No one could have secured a description, but because I'm chief of police and because I'm always yelling about keeping your presence of mind and getting a description of any car that acts suspicious—well, I don't need to draw a lot of diagrams for you. Now that's the situation."

"All right," I said. "You've been anxious to solve it. You've got evidence."

"You're damned right I've got evidence," he said.

"How much evidence?"

"Quite a bit. When the car hit me it smashed the right head-light. We have part of the lens. Some of the paint came off and we have a piece of grill—the stuff was from a Buick. If we could ever have found the damned car we could have made a case all right. But we couldn't find the car."

"You covered repair shops?"

"Of course I covered repair shops. What the hell! I had every repair shop that did any work on a car, particularly a Buick of that model, make a detailed report to the police."

"All right," I said, "then the accident was investigated."

"That's right."

I said, "Let's see if you have a report on work that was done on Holgate's automobile."

He studied my face for a minute, then began to grin. "Lam," he said, "there's just a chance—just a chance, mind you, that you're a lifesaver.

"I don't know as I'd buy this if it weren't for the fact that I am personally involved. It's a farfetched theory and I don't know, I have an idea you may be trying to cut yourself a piece of cake and get yourself out of a murder case.

"Before I look, I'm going to ask you one question. I want a frank answer. The authorities feel that you were in that place of Holgate's before you went back there with Holgate's secretary, apparently to discover the wreckage. Now, I'm going to give you one test question: Were you in there or weren't you?"

I looked him in the eyes and said, "I was in there."

"And then you went back the second time for a cover-up?"

"That's right."

"Why?"

"Because I didn't know what had happened, but I had made an affidavit that I'd seen that accident of Holgate's—"

"Why?" he asked.

"Because," I said, "I wanted to smoke the thing out in the open. I felt that if I made an affidavit that I'd seen the accident, that would start putting on pressure. You see, someone had been advertising for witnesses to that accident, offering first one hundred dollars and then boosting the ante to two hundred and fifty."

"Holgate, in desperation, trying to buy a perjured witness?" he asked.

"That was my theory, at first," I said, "but after I made the affidavit I was satisfied that it was someone who was trying to cover up for Holgate."

"Who would cover up for him?" he asked.

"Two people," I said. "One of them, his partner, and the other one, Vivian Deshler."

"His partner. You mean Chris Maxton?"

"That's right."

"And you think he might have?"

"There's evidence indicating he did. He paid me two hundred and fifty dollars when I convinced him that I'd been a witness to the accident."

Dale sat at his desk and thought things over. "You're rather unconventional and rather daring, Lam," he said. "You've stuck your neck into a lot of nooses trying to help a client."

"If my theory of what happened is right, my head will come out of the noose," I said.

"And if it isn't?"

"I'll get my damned neck broken," I told him.

"You sure will," he told me, and got up and went to a filing case. He pulled out a manila envelope, took it over to his desk and started pulling out papers.

"Hell, yes," he said, "the Holgate accident was reported, but our traffic department didn't look into it."

"Why?"

"Repairs were made in a garage in Los Angeles and the investigation was made over the telephone. The garage reported that it was a Buick automobile all right, but that the damages to the car were all accounted for, that both cars were in there being appraised by representatives of the Consolidated Interinsurance Company, and that all details of the accident had been verified, and the insurance company had admitted liability and ordered the cars fixed up."

"The detailed injuries were not described?"

"Sure, they were described," he said. "The whole front of the Buick car was caved in. Both headlights were smashed. All of the grill was gone."

I said, "If you want to keep anyone from identifying a hole in a garment, all you have to do is to take a pair of scissors and make the hole bigger. All Holgate had to do was to take a hammer and add to the injuries."

Dale said, "Lam, you fascinate the hell out of me. I'm not going to buy this wild-eyed theory of yours, but I'm sure as hell going to investigate it, and man, oh, man, how I hope you're right!"

I said, "You know there's a cover-up going on. When do you start investigating?"

"When do I start investigating?" he said. "Right now."

He dialed the phone again and said, "Sorry, honey, but I'm not going to be home. No, this is important. I can't tell you about it on the phone and...I'm sorry, you're just going to have to make apologies to the guests. They know that I'm on call twenty-four hours a day and this is one of those things....Atta girl, I knew you'd cooperate....You carry on and do the best you can."

He hung up the phone and said, "What's first?"

I said, "Chris Maxton. He's the one who put the ad in the paper offering two hundred and fifty dollars reward."

"Well, what's wrong with that? He was trying to help Holgate out."

I said, "Why help Holgate out?"

"Because Holgate was his partner."

I said, "What do you mean, help? Holgate had admitted liability to the insurance company. The insurance company had admitted liability to Vivian Deshler. Any witness to the accident could only have testified that it was Holgate's fault. So why the hell would he be helping Holgate out getting a witness?

"The only reason he could help Holgate out with a witness was because he knew the accident was phony and he was willing to offer a big enough bribe to get some person to perjure himself—"

"Let's go," Dale interrupted.

"Do you know where to find Chris Maxton?"

"Sure I do. He has an apartment here in town."

"Married?"

"Man about town," Dale said. "He plays around a bit, has some pretty good-looking babes on the string."

"Including Vivian Deshler?"

"Hell, I don't know," Dale said. "I've never cared enough to find out, but I'm going to make it my business to know now. Come on, Lam, let's go."

We got in the chief's automobile.

The chief drove conservatively for about three blocks. I

could see that he was thinking over my theory. The more he thought it over, the better he liked it.

At the end of three blocks he put on the red light. At the end of five blocks he turned on the siren.

Chief Dale was in a hurry.

We got to a rather swanky apartment house, and the chief parked his car in front of a fireplug, said, "Come on, Lam."

We went up in an elevator, and the chief pushed the mother-of-pearl button.

Chimes sounded on the inside.

Chris Maxton came to the door. He didn't see me for a moment but saw the chief.

"Why, hello, Chief," he said.

"I want to talk with you," Dale said.

Maxton was flustered. "I...I'm not alone...I—"

"I want to talk with you," Dale said.

"I...I have a young woman here. I—"

"I want to talk with you."

"Look," Maxton said, "give me just ten seconds to get her..."

Dale started in.

"Go in the bedroom, honey," Maxton called over his shoulder.

He said, "It's quite all right, Chief, but— What the hell, who's this with you?"

"Donald Lam," Dale said. "Do you know him?"

"Do I know him? The two-time chiseling, dirty crook! Why didn't you say this had to do with the case against Donald Lam? I'd do anything to nail that two-timing—"

"Take it easy," Dale said, pushing his way into the room. "You just answer questions."

"Well, I'm making a complaint. I'm having Donald Lam arrested for obtaining money under false pretenses and—"

"Save it, Chris," the chief said. "You just answer questions. What the hell's going on here?"

"Nothing," Chris said. "Oh, just a little sociable party." The chief looked around. There was a bottle of whiskey, some ice cubes, a couple of bottles of mixer, two empty glasses, a couple of women's shoes on the floor, a bra hanging over the back of a chair and a skirt rumpled into a corner.

Maxton said, "I'd just shut off the hi-fi when I heard the chimes."

"No, you didn't," Dale said, walking over to the window and looking out. "You shut off the hi-fi when you heard the siren. What the hell kind of a joint you running here?"

"Now, take it easy, Chief, take it easy," Maxton said.

I realized that the chief was getting him in the proper frame of mind, putting him sufficiently on the defensive so he'd spill everything he knew. It was a good job.

The chief went over to the corner, picked up the girl's skirt and looked at it. He walked over to the bra, looked at that, turned to the davenport, walked over and picked up a square box that had just been unwrapped. The wrapping paper was there on the floor.

The chief reached into the box, pulled out a pair of silk panties. There was lettering all over the silk. Lower down the lettering read: "THAT'S TOO FAR — NOW STOP — I'LL SLAP YOU."

Then up higher the lettering was: "WELL MAYBE — YES! YES! YES!"

"What the hell are these?" Dale asked.

Maxton said, "I sent away for them. They were advertised in one of the men's magazines as the ideal gift for the one girl-friend."

"I see," Dale said, "and you'd just talked the young lady into trying them on to see what they looked like?"

Maxton grinned sheepishly.

Chief Dale glowered at him, said suddenly and accusingly, "Why the hell did you advertise for witnesses to that accident?"

"I…I wanted to—well, I wanted to help my partner out."

"Cut out that crap," Dale told him, "or I'll open that door and run you both in for running an immoral party."

Chris spilled words out in a stream. "Well, you know how it is, Chief. My partner was involved in an accident and— Now look, Chief, you couldn't drag the young woman into this—and this is *my* apartment. I pay rent on it and—"

"To hell with that stuff," Dale said, "get back to the case. Why did you try to dig up a witness?"

Maxton took a long breath and said, "All right, I'll tell you why I tried to pick up a witness. I thought the accident was a phony."

Chief Dale sat down. His face softened. "*Now* you're beginning to talk," he said. "What made you think it was phony?"

Maxton said, "I knew damned well it was phony. Holgate's automobile was in good shape at four-thirty that afternoon. Whatever happened took place sometime after that.

"My partner had been drinking. He'd been involved in an automobile accident and he sure as hell was going to lots of trouble to cover it up."

"So what did *you* do?"

"I wanted to find out about it."

"By trying to bribe a witness to say he'd seen it?" Dale asked suspiciously.

"You don't get the sketch," Maxton said. "I wanted to prove that there *weren't* any witnesses. In that way I could prove there hadn't been any accident the way Holgate claimed. I intended to offer up to five thousand dollars to anyone who could prove that he'd seen the accident, but I wasn't going to stick my neck out all at once. I was going to make it a sure thing and play it up in such a dramatic way I'd cook Holgate's kettle of fish.

"I figured I'd start the ante at a hundred and then, when no witnesses showed up, I'd increase it to two fifty, then five hundred. Then, when no witnesses showed up, I'd make it a thousand. Then, with no witnesses, I'd make it two thousand. By that time I'd be sure of my ground and I'd have had the ads attracting so much attention that the insurance company would get suspicious and everyone would get suspicious."

"That's better," Dale said. "Why did you want everyone to get suspicious?"

"Because," Maxton said, "Holgate thought he had something on me and was trying to force me to sell out my interest in the partnership for less than it was worth. I just felt that I'd get something on that smug sonofabitch so he wouldn't be pushing me around. Now if you want to know, that's the truth."

"How did you know his car was in good shape at four-thirty in the afternoon?" Dale asked.

"I'd rather not go into that."

"And I want you to go into it."

"All right, his secretary told me."

"How did she know?"

"It was her birthday. There was a sort of office party and—"

"Cocktails?" Dale asked.

"Cocktails."

"Go on," Dale said. "What happened?"

"And then this cheap, chiseling, two-bit bastard, Donald Lam, got in the picture and told me such a convincing lie about having seen the accident that I came to the conclusion my suspicions were all wrong and I drew in my horns. I threw up my hands, decided I was licked and then paid the sonofabitch two hundred and fifty dollars in cash to boot."

Dale thought things over for a few moments, then he began to chuckle.

He got up and nodded to me. "Go on with your party," he said to Maxton. "I'm sorry I interrupted you and I hope the panties fit."

14

We went back down to the car. The chief started the motor. His eyes were narrowed in thoughtful speculation.

He turned on the radio and called in to the dispatcher. "This is Chief Dale in Car One. I'm working on a case. Anything new on that Holgate case? Over."

The dispatcher said, "Bulletin from the Los Angeles police just a few minutes ago, putting out an all points bulletin on Donald Lam. They've buttoned up the case against him and are ready to charge him with the murder of Carter Holgate. Over."

Chief Dale said, "Thanks. Keep in touch."

He shut off the radio and grinned at me.

"Your friend on the Los Angeles police force doesn't have much faith in you, does he?"

"Not much," I said. "How about making a telephone call?"

"Sure thing. Anything you want, Lam." He grinned again and said, "*Anything* you want. You name it, you can have it."

Then he began to chuckle.

"Some reason why Holgate wouldn't want to take the responsibility with you, Chief?" I asked.

"You're damned right there is," Dale said. "It's a long story. Holgate was high-pressure salesman. A good enough egg, but strictly high pressure. A friend of mine had some property up in the mountains. Holgate offered to trade it for a couple of lots in his subdivision. She went for it in a big way.

"After the trade had been made for about sixty days, it turned out there was a new highway going through the mountains and the location went right through the property this girl had owned. I don't know how much Holgate made out of it, but it was plenty."

"Did she do anything about it?" I asked.

"*She* didn't," Dale said. "But I had a talk with Holgate."

"What did he do?"

"He laughed at me."

"So," I said, "in case you were in a position to jail Holgate for drunk driving, hit-and-run...I'm beginning to see a great light."

"And *I'm* beginning to see a great light," Chief Dale said. "For your information, Lam, there's a special meeting of the council at nine-thirty this evening and one of the subjects on the agenda is getting a new police chief. When you dropped into my office it was manna from heaven. I hadn't told my wife about it because I didn't want to worry her. I was going to go home, have cocktails and dinner, and had made arrangements to be summoned on the telephone so I could go up to the council meeting and be available. But they hadn't invited me to be present. They were having an executive session and I gather my successor may have already been picked out sub rosa— Here's a good isolated telephone booth. Put through your call. Got all the money you need?"

"I have plenty," I said.

"Okay, I'll wait here."

The chief settled back in the car and lit a cigar. He was grinning like a Cheshire cat.

I put through a call to the office.

Bertha Cool answered. "Where the hell are you?" she said. "My God, do you know what's happened? That sonofabitch, Frank Sellers, let that Ace High Detective bastard sell him on the idea you were cutting corners. Heaven knows what sort of evidence they cooked up, but Sellers rang me up and told me to have you surrender yourself at once."

"What did you tell him?"

"I told him the truth. I told him you'd gone out and I didn't know where you were, and he said I had fifteen minutes to locate you and if I didn't locate you in that time he was putting out an all points bulletin, that he was tired of being made a patsy."

"Anything else?" I asked.

"That's it— Oh, wait a minute. Elsie wants to talk with you....Where the hell is she? She said she had something else that might interest you. I guess she's gone out."

"All right," I said. "Here's what I want you to do, Bertha. Get in your car and drive just as fast as you can to the Miramar Apartments in Colinda. You locate Elsie. Leave a message for her in her apartment house if you can't do anything else. Tell her to bring her scrapbook on automobile accidents and hit-and-run and get the hell out there just as fast as she can. I'll meet you there."

"How soon?"

"As soon as you get there."

"Do I get dinner first?" Bertha asked.

"Hell, no," I said. "You get out there just as fast as you can, and get Elsie out there."

I hung up the phone and started putting on an act. I'd pretend to drop a coin, then I'd dial a number. I kept that up for nearly ten minutes, pretending to talk and listen.

Chief Dale sat in the car, grinning. When he showed signs of getting restless I went out of the booth.

"Took you long enough," he said.

"I had several calls."

"All done?"

"All done, Chief."

"Well, Donald, I don't want to be hauled on the carpet for conspiring to protect a felon. You're wanted for murder. Hold out your wrists."

I held out my wrists. The chief snapped handcuffs on them. "You're under arrest," he said. "You're my prisoner. And I just want you to know that while you're my guest in the jail at Colinda, if there's any damned thing on earth you want, all you've got to do is to mention it. You can have special meals, special attention, a telephone in your cell, you can see anybody you want to. You can have anything you want except a dame. That I can't get for you."

"Thanks," I told him.

"Don't thank me," he said.

"Are you going to take me down to the jail before you—"

"Before I see Vivian Deshler?" he asked. "Hell, no. Don't think I'm dumb and don't be dumb yourself, Lam. I just put those handcuffs on you as a token. You're my prisoner—and you're too damned smart to try to escape. You may be innocent of the murder but after you've been placed under arrest by an officer, making an escape is a felony and—well, I wouldn't like that, Donald, and I could be awfully mean if something happened that I didn't like."

"I understand," I told him. "I'm sitting right here."

"Those handcuffs too tight?"

"No, they're very comfortable."

"Okay," he said. "Here we go."

We drove out to the Miramar Apartments, and the chief took me up in the elevator with him, handcuffs and all.

We went to Vivian Deshler's apartment.

The chief pushed his finger against the button and held it there until Vivian Deshler opened the door.

Dale pulled back his coat. "This is the police, Miss Deshler. I'm Chief Dale of Colinda, the chief of police."

"Oh, yes," she said. "What can I do for you, Chief?"

"I want to talk."

"Come in and sit down, Chief Dale," she said. "You're very welcome. I'm going out a little later but…"

The chief moved into the apartment and I followed him.

She saw me then and said, "Well, just a moment. I didn't know you had a guest."

"He isn't my guest," Chief Dale said. "He's my prisoner. He's under arrest for the murder of Carter Holgate."

"Good heavens," she said. "He's under arrest! Why, I knew they were investigating him and—"

"He's under arrest," Dale said.

"Donald," she said, "I'm sorry! I didn't mean to rub it in. I— Well, you can understand."

I said, "It's quite all right," and sat down, putting my elbows on my legs so that the bright reading lamp shone down on the manacles on my wrists.

"I'm investigating this accident of yours," Chief Dale said. "The one where Carter Holgate is supposed to have bumped into the rear of your car and—"

She drew herself up and said, "I am not going to be questioned any more about that accident, Chief Dale. I have talked about it until I'm sick and tired of it. I have a claim against the insurance company, I have now retained an attorney, I have decided to file suit. My attorney has advised me to say nothing about it."

Dale said patiently, "I understand. That's looking at it from the standpoint of a civil action. But now I'm looking at it from the standpoint of a criminal action."

"What do you mean?"

Dale said, "I now have pretty good evidence that Carter Holgate smashed into my car on the evening of the thirteenth of August. He was driving while he was drunk."

"For heaven's sake," she said.

"Now, that accident occurred a little after five-thirty in the evening," Chief Dale said.

"Well, what do you know!"

"That's exactly it," Dale said. "I know so much that I want to know a little more. In fact I want to know *quite* a little more."

She was doing some fast thinking.

"That must have been his day for accidents," she said.

"Now," Dale said, "I want to know about his accident with you. I want to know about when he hit your car."

"Well, to be perfectly frank with you, Chief, I'm not certain of the hour. I am of the date but—"

"Was it after dark?"

"No, no. It was in the afternoon. It was— I just can't go back in my mind right at this time and pinpoint the exact hour."

I said, "Her friend, Doris Ashley, saw her car about three-thirty or three-forty-five and it had been smashed at that time, so the accident must have taken place before then, Chief."

Vivian flashed me a look of pure venom.

"That right?" he asked Vivian.

"I wouldn't know. Anything Doris says—she's a very truthful girl and quite observant."

"Now, I'm going to be fair with you, Miss Deshler," Dale said. "If Holgate hit my car, pushed it into the ditch, then drove on, that would be a crime. That's a hit-and-run. You understand that?"

"Why, yes, of course."

"And," Dale went on, "if anybody conspired with him to cover up that crime or help him escape the penalty, that person would be an accessory after the fact and would be guilty of lots of things—not only guilty of the crime as an accessory, but guilty of criminal conspiracy. Do you understand that?"

She wet her lips with the tip of her tongue.

"Yes," she said after a moment.

"Now under those circumstances," Dale said, "would you have any statement to make to me, Miss Deshler?"

"I...I know that— Now, wait a minute, let me think....I'm sorry, but would you excuse me for a moment, please? I haven't been feeling well lately. I have to go to the bathroom. I'll be right back."

She got up and vanished through a door in the apartment.

Dale winked at me and then got up and tiptoed to the closed door. He took a little microphone attachment from his pocket, put it up against the door, put earphones in his ears, snapped on a switch and listened.

A grin came over his face as he listened.

He looked at me and winked once more, then kept listening for what must have been two or three minutes.

Suddenly he jerked the earphones out of his ears, detached the device from the door, slipped it into his pocket, tiptoed back to his chair and seated himself.

The door from the bedroom opened. Vivian Deshler said, "I'm sorry to have been so abrupt but I'm having some kind of an intestinal upset and— Well, I hope you don't think I'm unladylike."

"Not at all," Dale said.

"Now, just what was it you wanted to know, Chief?"

"About that accident."

"Oh, yes. Well, I've made a statement to the insurance company. I've made statements to the police, I've made statements to investigators, I've…I've just made so many statements I'm sick to death of that accident.

"I'll tell you what I'm going to do, Chief Dale. I was injured in that accident. I had what they call a whiplash injury and I understand that can be very serious, but I'm just so sick and tired of the whole business that I've decided to absorb the loss myself. I'm going to withdraw my claim against the insurance company and forget the whole business. I'm going to go away and try to rest. My doctor thinks that complete rest with nothing to worry about may do a great deal to restore me to health."

She looked at me. I twisted my arm so that the light reflected from the handcuffs. She stared at them with fascination.

"Well, that's all very nice," Dale said. "I hope you recover your health. I might tell you, Miss Deshler, that this means a good deal to me, getting this case solved, because you see my car was pushed into the ditch by a hit-and-run driver. I now have reason to believe that driver was Carter Holgate and that he used this purely imaginary accident he had had with your car to cover up—"

"What do you mean, an imaginary accident?" she asked with cold dignity. "There's no reason he couldn't have been in two accidents. If he was drunk—"

"I mean exactly what I said," Dale interrupted, "that the accident was wholly imaginary."

"Well, I like that!" she said. "Are you accusing me of lying?"

"Frankly," Dale said, "I'm accusing you of lying, Miss Deshler. I'm accusing you of having faked the accident to your car and of having conspired with Holgate to involve your car in an accident with him. That was designed to get Holgate off the spot and, in case you're interested, I used a listening device when you were supposedly in the bathroom with your intestinal upset.

"You telephoned someone and asked him for advice as to what to do. Now, who was it?"

"That," she said, "was my lawyer and you have absolutely no right to eavesdrop on a conversation with a lawyer. I am going to ask you to leave my apartment."

"I'll leave if you insist," Dale said, "but when I leave it's a declaration of war. I'm giving you a chance now to come clean."

"What do you mean, come clean?"

"To tell me the truth."

"What do you mean you're...giving me a chance?"

"If you tell the story now," Dale said, "I'll give you the breaks. If you don't, I'll throw the book at you."

She bit her lip, hesitated for a moment, then shook her head. "There's nothing to tell."

"I think there is."

She hesitated a moment, then said, "All right, if you want the truth, I'll tell you the truth."

"That's better."

She said, "It all gets back to this man that you have with you, this Donald Lam."

"And how does he enter into the picture?"

"He enters into it in this way. He's trying to protect the insurance company that hired him. He bribed Lorraine Robbins, Mr. Holgate's secretary, to say that she saw Holgate's automobile after four o'clock, and that it was all right. He's left a dirty, slimy trail of corruption all through this case. He's resorted to intimidation of witnesses, he's resorted to bribery, and he's committed downright perjury.

"He's sworn that he was a witness to the accident and he wasn't a witness at all....That accident took place just as I have described it and if you want to throw your weight around and browbeat somebody, you go get Lorraine Robbins and start working on her and you'll find out that Donald Lam and she have been in cahoots on this thing all the way through.

"And if you want to know, Donald Lam was out there at Holgate's place before he ever got in touch with Lorraine Robbins and lured her out there with the excuse that they should look for Carter Holgate. I think he has an accomplice. I don't know who that accomplice was, but those are the facts in the case and I'm not going to be pushed around by any murderer who is trying to clear his own skirts at my expense.

"Now you'll pardon me, Chief Dale, but that's the last statement I intend to make. I hadn't intended to go that far because I don't want to accuse anyone else of crime. I believe in living and let live, but I've been crowded just too far. I am now going to consult my attorney and I'm not going to make any other statement to you or anyone else except in the presence of my attorney."

She got up and said, "I'm sorry to be abrupt, Chief Dale, but this interview is terminated."

Dale said, "Don't let yourself get all worked up, Miss Deshler. I'm just trying—"

"I'm sorry, but you have questioned my word and I am now satisfied that this whole case has been stirred up by Mr. Lam, who has obtained money under false pretenses, who has made false affidavits, who has tried every dirty, sneaky trick in the quiver in order to discredit me and in order to get the insurance company that retained him off the hook.

"I'm surprised that an officer of your experience would fall for this type of thing. You certainly should consider his interests in the case and what he is trying to do. He is a murderer who is trying to draw red herrings across the trail, and you have fallen for one of the oldest tricks in the whole history of investigative work. And now if you'll excuse me. I'm...I'm going to the bathroom again."

She made a run for the door, slammed it shut and locked it.

Dale looked at me. I could see doubt creeping into his eyes.

"You going to let her get away with that?"

"Hell's bells, what are you going to do?" Dale said. "She said she was going to the bathroom. This time she's smart enough to go there. She locked the door. I can't smash the door down and drag her out of the bathroom. I haven't any warrant. I haven't even anything to go on—except *your* word!"

He looked at me again and said, "Come on, Lam. I guess we'll go down to headquarters. I'll have to notify Los Angeles that I have you in custody."

We walked over and he opened the door. "Come on."

I followed him out into the corridor.

"When you come right down to it," he said, "your theory stinks."

"Why does it stink?"

"What incentive did Vivian Deshler have to fake an accident with Carter Holgate?"

"A whiplash injury," I said. "Look into her past and I don't doubt you'll find she's been in an automobile accident before, claimed a whiplash injury and received a damned good settlement from some insurance company."

"Could be," Dale said, his voice indicating he wasn't particularly interested.

He led the way to the elevator.

"I'm going to think over your theory of this thing, Lam, and I'm going to talk with this Lorraine Robbins."

"She's here in this apartment house," I said. "You might just as well make a good job of it while you're doing it."

"She lives here?"

"That's right."

"Okay," Dale said. "We'll talk with her. But I don't mind telling you right now, Donald, that I'm sorry I got the cart before the horse on this thing. I should have talked with her first before I went in and tried to get rough with Vivian Deshler.

"She's in a position to make quite a squawk if she gets an attorney. I accused her of faking an accident, all on the strength of a theory you had, and your theory is supported on what you say Lorraine Robbins told you.

"I guess my personal interest clouded my judgment a little bit."

I said, "All right, come on, let's go talk with Lorraine Robbins."

"You, Lam, are going down and sit in my automobile. You're going to be handcuffed to the steering wheel. I don't want you to try any funny stuff. For your information, your stock has taken a sharp nose dive in the last fifteen minutes."

He took me back down to the automobile, handcuffed me to the steering wheel, went back to the apartment house.

Minutes passed. Ten minutes became fifteen minutes.

A car drew up, looked around for a parking place, finally found one.

I twisted around as much as the handcuffs would let me.

Bertha Cool and Elsie Brand got out.

Elsie was carrying a scrapbook.

"Bertha!" I shouted.

She didn't hear me.

"Elsie!" I yelled.

Elsie looked up and looked around.

"Over here, Elsie!"

Elsie saw me then and came running.

"Why, Donald—what is it? Whatever's happened?"

Bertha came waddling up behind, took a look at the handcuffs and said, "So they found you."

"They found me," I said. "What did you want to see me about, Elsie? What was the news?"

She said, "Something in one of the scrapbooks, Donald—Oh, I hope it will help!"

"All right, what is it?"

She said, "The stick-up of that bank out in North Hollywood where they got away with forty thousand dollars. The getaway car was some kind of a sports car and no one got a very good look at it, but one of the witnesses said the hind end had been damaged. It had a big dent of some sort in it. It—"

"When was it, when was it, Elsie?" I asked, interrupting her.

"Just shortly before closing time on the thirteenth."

I turned to Bertha. "You get the hell up to Apartment six-nineteen in the Miramar Apartments. Vivian Deshler is in there. Either she was mixed up in that bank robbery or her car was. That explains the mystery. That's the reason she was willing to ride along with Holgate. Now remember, there *has* to be some connection. Somebody that knew Holgate's car was smashed had to know that the tail end of her car was caved in and she needed an explanation for that quick. Otherwise she'd have been connected with that bank robbery or her car would have been."

Bertha blinked at me a couple of times, then turned and started for the apartment house.

"You want Elsie with you?" I asked.

"Hell, no," she said. "I don't need any help and I don't want any witnesses."

Elsie said, "You poor boy," and climbed into the car beside me.

She'd been in the car about five minutes when Chief Dale came out and started walking thoughtfully over to the car.

"Hello," he said, stopping suddenly and his hand dropping to his hip. "What's all this?"

"This, Chief," I said, "is my secretary, Elsie Brand. She saves interesting newspaper clippings of unsolved crimes."

"All right," he said. "What's it all about? Now, just a minute, Miss Brand, this man is my prisoner. Don't try to give him anything, don't try to release those handcuffs."

"I think you're horrid," Elsie said to him. "The idea of suspecting—"

"Take it easy, Elsie," I said. "Show Chief Dale the clipping you were telling me about."

Elsie squirmed out of the car, opened the scrapbook and pointed out the clipping to Chief Dale.

Dale leaned forward to read it. He read it once, looked up, squinted his eyes thoughtfully, then read it twice.

Then he said, "I'll be damned!"

There was a long silence.

"How did you come out in there with Lorraine Robbins?" I asked.

"Lam," he said, "she's on the up and up. She's a good kid. There's something fishy about that accident just as sure as hell. Holgate's car was all right at four-thirty on the thirteenth."

"And," I said, "Vivian Deshler's car had the rear end caved in at three-thirty on the thirteenth."

"By God, if it all *does* tie in! If Holgate was the hit-and-run guy and if that Deshler car was the getaway car in that bank robbery— Good God Almighty, what *that* would do!"

I said, "Be a pretty nice thing to clean all that mess up and walk in on the meeting of the city council at nine-thirty, wouldn't it, Chief? You could show them that you'd cleared up the mystery of the hit-and-run driver, that you'd solved the bank robbery and—"

"All right," he said. "I've fallen for it once. I'll fall for it twice. I'm going back up."

"Better take me with you," I said.

He shook his head.

"You may need a witness."

He thought that over.

"Two witnesses," Elsie said.

"You take shorthand?" Dale asked.

She nodded.

"All right, come on," he said.

He unlocked the handcuff that was holding me to the steering wheel, hesitated a moment, then snapped the handcuff back on my wrist. "Remember," he said, "you're still under arrest. I'm investigating this damned story but I'm not buying it. Not yet. I'm window shopping."

We started toward the entrance to the apartment house.

I stalled things along as much as I could but eventually we got into the elevator and got up to the sixth floor.

As we walked down the corridor I could hear sounds of banging and thumping.

A woman screamed.

"What's that?" Chief Dale asked.

I made my last stall. "It came from that apartment over there," I said.

"I thought it came from farther down the line," Dale said.

"No, I'm quite certain it was this apartment," I said, and caught Elsie Brand's eye.

"It came from this one right here," she said.

Dale hesitated a moment, then went over and banged on the door of the apartment.

There was no answer.

He banged again.

After a moment a woman who had some kind of a robe hastily thrown around her shoulders, and who seemed to be completely nude except for that, opened the door a crack. "Well," she snapped, "what is it?"

"Police," Dale said. "We're investigating a disturbance."

"There's no disturbance here."

"Didn't you scream?"

"I certainly did not."

Dale said, "I beg your—"

The door was slammed in his face.

Dale looked at me and said, "I'm beginning to know how the Los Angeles officers feel about you, Lam. You knew damned well those sounds didn't come from that apartment. What are you stalling for?"

I said, "I could have been mistaken."

"And you could have been playing games," Dale said.

He strode on down to 519 and pressed the mother-of-pearl button. Nothing happened.

After a moment he banged on the door with his knuckles, a hard, peremptory police knock. "Open up!" he said.

There was a moment of silence, then the door was jerked open.

Bertha Cool, her face flushed, said, "Well, come on in! Don't stand there in the hallway gawking."

Vivian Deshler was standing over in a corner sobbing hysterically. Her skirt had been ripped completely off. She was standing there in bra and panties, and the panties were embroidered with fancy mottos: "THAT'S TOO FAR—NOW STOP—I'LL SLAP YOU—WELL MAYBE—YES! YES! YES!"

"Who are you?" Dale asked Bertha Cool.

"I'm Bertha Cool, Donald Lam's partner," she said, "and this little bitch is going to make a confession to you about being mixed up with a man by the name of Dudley Bedford in a bank robbery out in North Hollywood. They got about forty thousand dollars in cash and it's somewhere in the apartment here. Where is it, dearie?"

Vivian Deshler put her hands in front of her eyes. "You stop!" she said.

Bertha Cool moved toward her. "Where is it, dearie?"

"In the suitcase in the closet!" she screamed. "Don't you touch me! Don't you dare!"

"Look in the suitcase in the closet," Bertha Cool said matter-of-factly, and walked over to the closet, took out a coat and tossed it to Vivian Deshler.

"Stick this around you in case you feel self-conscious," she said.

Dale looked at Bertha, looked at Vivian Deshler, looked at me. "And who murdered Holgate?" he asked.

"Do you need to ask?" I said. "You've seen those panties before, you know. She could get plenty of information out of Maxton—the cocktail party and all the rest of the background she needed."

Dale said to Bertha Cool, "Can you keep her from trying to escape?"

"I can keep *her* from so much as flapping an eyelash," Bertha said. "She tries to pull out on me and I'll slap her to sleep."

"You're deputized," Chief Dale barked. "I'm going to take a look in that suitcase."

He was back in two minutes with the suitcase opened and looking at the money all neatly arranged in packages.

It was at that moment a latchkey sounded in the door of the apartment.

Vivian Deshler sucked in a deep breath to scream a warning.

Bertha Cool slapped her in the stomach and knocked the wind out of her. She doubled up like an accordion.

The door clicked back and a smiling, debonair Dudley Bedford came marching into the room.

He took one look at what was happening and went for his gun.

Dale beat him to the punch. "You're under arrest," he snapped. "Get your hands up."

Bedford slowly elevated his hands.

"Turn around, face the wall," Dale ordered. "Now stick your hands out behind you."

Bedford did as he was instructed.

Dale came over, unlocked the handcuffs from my wrists, put them on Bedford's wrists, looked at me, grinned, looked at his watch, said to Bertha, "You're deputized as a matron. Get some clothes on that prisoner and get her up to the station house. I'm in a hurry. I want to get a complete confession out of these people and I want to have it by nine-thirty."

Bertha said, "Get some clothes out of the closet, dearie, and you'd better take those ornamental panties off. Where you're going, nobody gives a damn about smart mottos embroidered on fannies."

15

It was ten-fifteen when Chief Dale emerged from the council meeting, strode over to the telephone, picked it up and said, "Get me police headquarters in Los Angeles. I want to talk with Sergeant Frank Sellers."

He looked at me and winked.

It took about two minutes for the call to get through, then Dale said, "Hello, Sellers?

"This is Montague Dale. I'm the chief of police at Colinda. I have Donald Lam. I understand that there's an all points bulletin out for him."

Dale listened for a while and grinned.

After a moment he said, "Well, before you stick your neck out, Sergeant, you probably should know that there wasn't any automobile accident with Holgate. That thing was all cooked up. Holgate sideswiped a police car on the evening of the thirteenth when he was drunk, and wanted to get out from under. A man by the name of Bedford, who was friendly with Holgate, learned what had happened and advised Holgate to fake an accident with a friend of his, a Vivian Deshler, so that he could account for the broken front of his automobile. Vivian was also a friend of Maxton, Holgate's partner.

"It looked like a good deal to Holgate, who didn't know what he was getting into, but Vivian Deshler, who had previously made a couple of claims against insurance companies on whiplash injuries, tried to shake the insurance company down for thirty grand.

"Her car had been cracked earlier in the day when she lost

control of it and backed into an ornamental lighting pole in North Hollywood. At the time she was on her way with her boyfriend, Dudley Bedford, to rob a bank in North Hollywood. They cleaned it up to the tune of more than forty grand.

"Thanks to the cooperation of Donald Lam, who gave me the leads which cracked the case, I have just recovered the money and obtained complete confessions from all concerned.

"I don't think Holgate ever did know that he was being suckered into a bank robbery, but he knew that the girl was making a claim for whiplash injuries against the insurance company and that scared the hell out of him. When Lam showed up to make an affidavit that he had seen the accident, he knew, of course, that Lam was lying and figured that Lam had been procured by Bedford and that Lam's affidavit put Holgate in the position of suborning perjury.

"So Holgate decided to make a complete confession of the whole business. He went up to his office, turned on the electric typewriter, telephoned for Lam to come out there and started tapping out a written statement.

"In the meantime, Dudley Bedford had found out what was going on. As soon as his detective agency found out Donald Lam wasn't an ex-convict who had been released from San Quentin, they knew the fat was in the fire—so Bedford and Vivian Deshler went out to Holgate's place of business, where they found him tapping out a confession.

"There was a hell of a fight and they knocked Holgate out. Then they read the confession and confiscated it. They dragged Holgate out to their car.

"They looked around for Lam's affidavit and found it. They did a little searching to see if Holgate had made any other written statements, then they went away. The girl drove Holgate's car. Bedford drove his car with the unconscious Holgate in it. They tied up Holgate hand and foot, then Bedford left him with the girl and Bedford drove back to the office to retrieve the report from his detective agency which had spilled out of the girl's broken purse and which she realized she had neglected to recover.

"Bedford found Donald Lam in the office going through things. Lam ducked out of the window and made his escape.

"They knew then they were in over their neckties. There was only one thing for them to do and that was to kill Holgate, plant his body in Donald Lam's car and frame Lam for the murder.

"I guess you can't be blamed for falling for it, Sergeant, because it was a pretty good frame-up, but Lam came to me and gave me a lot of help in buttoning the thing up.

"Vivian Deshler, of course, wanted to be in the clear on the murder so she took a plane back to Salt Lake City, boarded a transcontinental plane at Salt Lake and pretended she had just arrived from New York, thereby giving herself an alibi of sorts.

"I have complete confessions.

"Doris Ashley, who knew that Vivian Deshler's car had been damaged as early as three-thirty, having seen the car right after the completion of the bank robbery, was a troublesome witness. They had a detective agency shadow her to see if she suspected anything and was going to the police, and they had Dudley Bedford get intimate with her so he could see she didn't suspect anything.

"Now, I have Donald Lam here and if you insist on holding him I'll hold him but…"

Chief Dale listened for about two or three minutes.

Then as the receiver ceased making squawking noises, Dale laughed and said, "Well, of course, that's *your* hard luck, Sergeant. But it just happens that *I* could use a little good luck. I was in a little trouble here with the city council.…No, it's nothing to worry about. In fact it's all fixed up now. I've just been retained at a handsome increase in salary and I've been given to understand that I can have the five new officers I've been asking for, the two new patrol cars I want, and just about anything else I need. And I can keep the ten grand reward offered on the bank job. I'm doing all right.

"Shall I tell Donald Lam anything for you?"

Again Dale listened and a grin wrapped his face from ear to ear. "Okay," he said, and hung up.

He turned to me, extended his hand, gripped mine and pumped it up and down.

"The sergeant had a message for me?" I asked.

"Two words," he said. "Drop dead."